Emily dropped a kiss on her mother's cheek. 'Isn't it fun having Dad around?' she whispered, and suddenly Clare's spring of happiness wasn't bubbling quite as high.

She knew it wasn't jealousy she was feeling, but disappointment of some kind—disappointment that the life she'd been providing for her daughter hadn't measured up...

'You need my pearls—the ones Gran gave me,' Emily declared as she inspected her mother for the last time. 'Wait here.'

She ran off to her bedroom and returned with the pearls that had been her great-grandmother's, making her mother sit on the bed so she, Emily, could fasten them.

'There,' she said, 'you're beautiful. Dad will surely want to marry you now.'

Clare knew the words were nothing more than childish enthusiasm, but once again the joy of the morning dimmed, and despair wormed its way into her heart.

How could she resist if it became a matter of two against one?

CHRISTMAS AT JIMMIE'S

At Jimmie's Children's Unit,
miracles don't just happen at Christmas
time—babies are saved every day!

But this year there are two children
with some big wishes for Santa…

BACHELOR OF THE BABY WARD
—little Hamish McDowell
wants a new mummy…

FAIRYTALE ON THE CHILDREN'S WARD
—all Emily Jackson longs for
is to see her mum and dad reunited…

*Will Hamish and Emily
get the greatest Christmas gifts of all?*

Find out in Meredith Webber's heartwarming
linked duet, out this month!

FAIRYTALE ON THE CHILDREN'S WARD

BY
MEREDITH WEBBER

First published in Great Britain 2010
Large Print edition 2011
Harlequin Mills & Boon Limited,
Eton House, 18-24 Paradise Road,
Richmond, Surrey TW9 1SR

© Meredith Webber 2010

ISBN: 978 0 263 21729 2

Harlequin Mills & Boon policy is to use papers that are
natural, renewable and recyclable products and made
from wood grown in sustainable forests. The logging and
manufacturing process conform to the legal environmental
regulations of the country of origin.

Printed and bound in Great Britain
by CPI Antony Rowe, Chippenham, Wiltshire

Meredith Webber says of herself, 'Some ten years ago, I read an article which suggested that Mills and Boon were looking for new Medical™ Romance authors. I had one of those "I can do that" moments, and gave it a try. What began as a challenge has become an obsession—though I do temper the "butt on seat" career of writing with dirty but healthy outdoor pursuits, fossicking through the Australian Outback in search of gold or opals. Having had some success in all of these endeavours, I now consider I've found the perfect lifestyle.'

Recent titles by the same author:

DESERT KING, DOCTOR DADDY
GREEK DOCTOR: ONE MAGICAL CHRISTMAS
CHILDREN'S DOCTOR, MEANT-TO-BE WIFE*
THE HEART SURGEON'S SECRET CHILD†

*Crocodile Creek
†Jimmie's Children's Unit

CHAPTER ONE

OLIVER RANKIN hated being late. He was a man who believed there were no acceptable excuses for it, and condemned the rudeness of it. But he was undoubtedly running late, due mainly to car trouble on his drive from Melbourne to Sydney—trouble that had delayed him twenty-four hours while a part was sent, apparently by camel train, from Melbourne to the Victorian border.

Then there was Sydney peak-hour traffic—unbelievable!

Eventually, however, the latest fellow appointed to Alex Attwood's paediatric cardiac surgical team pulled into the parking lot at St James Hospital for Children, abandoned his car in a board-members-only parking spot and raced into the building.

Fortunately he'd spent a month with the team

earlier in the year so he knew where to go, but he still only made the meeting with a couple of seconds to spare.

Relief swamped him!

Until—

The world whirled before his eyes. Low blood pressure—all the rushing…

He dropped into a chair as Alex introduced him to Angus, the new surgeon on the team, and reminded him he'd already met Kate. Then he closed his eyes, and opened them again.

Carefully.

The apparition had come right into the room, later than he was.

A totally beautiful, totally mind-blowing apparition…

'And this is Clare Jackson, our new perfusionist,' Oliver heard Alex say. 'I'm more delighted than I can tell you to welcome Clare to our team as she trained in the US at the same hospital as Theo, and the oldies on the team will know how good he was.'

Oliver battled to sort out the disbelief in his head, to actually accept that the woman who still, from time to time, haunted his dreams was right here in this room.

Impossible!

Except it wasn't! There she was, head tilted towards Alex, so he saw her in profile, and caught the long line of her neck—the neck he'd loved to—

Clare Jackson?

He'd had the list of team members' names for a couple of weeks, but as she'd shown up on that as C. Jackson and most perfusionists he'd worked with had been males, he hadn't given a thought to the coincidence of surnames.

Alex was talking, but the words didn't penetrate Oliver's brain. Not only was Clare right here in this room, but apparently she was a team member. He'd be working with her.

She was a *perfusionist*?

From actress to lifesaving medical equipment expert in ten short years?

'Clare!' he'd managed to blurt out when they'd been introduced.

She'd nodded, lustrous dark hair swirling around her head, brown eyes half hooded, long eyelashes hiding any emotion those eyes might reveal at this unexpected reunion.

'Oliver,' she'd said, her voice still so familiar a tremor of excitement had shaken his body.

He tried to concentrate on Alex's introductions to the rest of the team, but how could he? He snuck a glance at Clare, and was annoyed to see that *she* seemed totally unfazed by this incredible coincidence.

Clare held her body very still, glad she'd learned how to do this years ago—back when she was a drama student at university, back when she'd first met Oliver.

Besides, if she held her body very still it might not fall apart, which was what it was threatening to do any moment.

Her body *and* her mind!

That he should be here—on the same team—was so unbelievable she had to wonder if it was some giant conspiracy of the Fates. Of course, even ten years ago, Oliver had been headed for a paediatric specialty, but he'd never mentioned surgery.

Whatever, it was indisputably Oliver sitting on the other side of the room, ignoring her in the politest possible way. Although what could he have said?

Long time, no see?

Not for Oliver the trite phrase, nor even idle conversation. The problem was that eventually the meeting would end and they would have to leave the room and *some* kind of conversation would obviously have to take place!

He'd come to claim Emily!

Nausea roiled in her stomach as the thought struck like the flick of a whip, but common sense prevailed. He'd obviously been as shocked to see her as she was to see him, and if he'd wanted his child surely he'd have got in touch back when she'd told him about the pregnancy.

Or in the intervening years?

And the fact that he hadn't—that he obviously *didn't* want to know his daughter—hardened her heart against him once again.

She could handle this! She could handle *anything*!

Easy to think, harder to do. Fear for her

daughter fluttered in her heart, fear for Em's emotional stability.

Her mind ran wild.

Now he *was* here, wouldn't he *want* to see his daughter—to get to know her?

And if he still refused to acknowledge her, how would that affect Em?

Thinking about her daughter opened up a void so deep and black Clare felt as if she was teetering on a precipice, about to be plunged into a bottomless abyss.

Yet how could she *not* think of Emily, *not* put her first?

She'd have to talk to Oliver, find out what he wanted and whether Emily was part of it. Then she—perhaps they—could work out how to get father and daughter together—or not—with the least possible upheaval in Emily's life.

She sneaked another glance at the man causing such havoc in her mind, and this time felt her heart turn over. Silver threads had infiltrated his sandy hair at both temples, lending him an air of distinction, but Oliver had always been a distinguished-looking man—tall, lean, tanned, with dark brows above those startling pale green eyes. In profile slightly hawkish, the long thin nose tipped down just slightly at the end.

Pointing to his lips?

That had been a stupid fantasy of hers in her youth, for Oliver Rankin had the most beautiful mouth she'd ever seen, on a man or woman.

Oliver!

Huge inward sigh!

She tried to concentrate on Alex's words, but her mind was way back in the past.

With Oliver...

How had things gone so disastrously wrong between them? How had she been stupid enough to walk out on him?

Because he didn't want the child you yearned for, she reminded herself. Didn't want a child at all and definitely not right then for all it would have been an ideal time as far as you were concerned. But part of the stupidity had been thinking he'd come after you, and that somehow the two of you could have patched things up.

That hadn't happened!

She'd spent a miserable Christmas at home on the farm with her family, then the realisation had dawned that, wanted or not, she was going to have a baby.

Tentative delight…

Quickly quelled at the thought of Oliver's reaction.

Which hadn't come!

Unable to contact him by phone or email, she'd finally written, but when he hadn't answered her letters—had ignored her unexpected news—she'd decided she'd have to forget all about him, which, she'd admitted to herself even then, was easier said than done. Until the diagnosis of her father's illness had turned her family's life upside down and concern and grief for him had swamped the pain of losing Oliver. Then, within weeks of Em's birth, life had changed so irrevocably Oliver had been the last person she'd been thinking of.

No, that was wrong. She'd longed for him—for his presence, his support, to have him there to share her dread and fear.…

And not having him, she'd turned to the man who *was* there—

She shuddered as she shook the memory away, and concentrated on what Alex Attwood, the team leader, was saying.

'Oliver, Kate and Clare, you'll all be working with Angus tomorrow. Clare, I know you've settled into your flat, so maybe you could show Oliver where his is. Did I tell you he's taking the other flat in Rod's house?'

Of course Alex hadn't told her! Excited as she'd been at coming back to Australia and getting a job in such an elite unit, she'd still have remembered if someone had said, Oh, and a chap called Oliver Rankin will be living next door! Not only remembered, but packed up and left.

No, she didn't run from men any more, but she'd have had time to at least think about this situation, to prepare herself.

To prepare Emily?

Oh, sweet reason, *what* was she going to do about Emily? For one crazy moment she thought of phoning the school and asking if they could take her as a full boarder rather than a weekly one, but it was hard enough on both of them to be separated five days a week.

Alex had turned to Oliver, and was explaining. 'The flat I arranged for you is in my father-in-law's house just down the road from the hospital. Rod Talbot, my father-in-law, is in a wheelchair so he has the ground-floor apartment and has turned upstairs into two small but comfortable flats. Of course, you don't have to stay there. Once you get to know the area, you might find somewhere that suits you better. Because of the proximity to the hospital, the flats are easy to let—not that Rod needs the money.'

'Rod Talbot?' Oliver repeated, his voice stirring so many memories in Clare's body she found herself shivering. 'Is he the writer?'

Alex nodded, and while Oliver talked about how much he enjoyed Rod Talbot's books— Oliver having time to read?—Clare muddled over the other information she'd received. The bit about Oliver being in the other flat in Rod Talbot's house—the flat with the door right opposite her door. Oliver living so close, sleeping so close...

A tremor of memory ran through her body before she brought her mind firmly back to the major problem.

Oliver spending his weekends next door to her and Emily!

Once again her reaction was flight. They'd go back to the States; she'd always find work there. But she steeled herself against such weakness— flight *wasn't* an option. She wasn't an emotional young woman any longer; she was a grown-up, mature—a qualified and respected career woman with an important position in a team that saved children's lives.

Even if she *did* feel like a teenager right now, with all the confusion and angst and dreadful insecurity that came with the transition from child to adult.

The meeting was breaking up, the anaesthetist from the second team taking the new surgeon off to the childcare centre. Dear heaven, had Oliver married again? Would he have children?

No, he'd been adamant about that, about never having children. That was why they'd split up. To a certain extent Clare had understood, because it had been soon after he'd found out a little about his own past, found out his life had been built upon a lie.

Thinking about that time—how hurt Oliver had been—diverted her thoughts from Oliver's marital arrangements, although if there *was* a wife, what would *she* think about Em?

It was all Clare could do not to wail out loud. How could this be happening to her? And now, when both she and Em were so excited to be back in Australia?

She pulled herself together with an effort.

Best not to think about Em! Not here, not now…

And it was useless to be speculating about Oliver's marital state, let alone whether he had children or not, although Rod had told Clare hers was the larger of the two flats, so a wife and children could hardly fit into the other one.

This realisation made her feel a little easier

for all of five seconds, until it occurred to her he could have left his wife and kids—if he'd weakened on the children stand—in Melbourne while he settled in.

'Clare.'

Her name in his voice, a sound she'd never thought to hear again. *No-one* said her name as Oliver did! And no-one else, with just that one word, could send those stupid shivers down her spine.

After ten years?

It was unbelievable.

She'd heard of muscle memory—sportspeople talked about it. Was there such a thing as nerve memory, that every nerve in her body remembered…?

He was close now, waiting for her. The composure he wore like a well-cut suit to hide the emotional Italian inside him was so familiar she wanted to reach out and touch him, to feel the warmth of the man beneath that cool facade.

Was she mad?

Touching Oliver would be disastrous—had

always been disastrous!—because one touch had never been enough.

She dug through her memory for an image of that last morning, not long before Christmas, when, all composure gone, fury and resentment had flared from his body and burnt in his eyes. That was the Oliver she needed to keep in mind.

Which was okay as far as resisting his appeal went, but what about the rest? What about Emily?

Clare felt physically sick, nausea spreading through her body. How could this have happened? She pulled herself together with a mammoth effort, hoping outwardly at least she might look composed.

'So we're to be neighbours,' she said, offering a polite smile, while her bewildered heart beat a wild tattoo inside her chest, and her thoughts ran this way and that like mice in a maze.

'It seems that way.'

Were his words strained? Was Oliver feeling the same mix of disbelief, and confusion—and surely not excitement?—as she was?

Of course he wouldn't be. For one thing, Oliver didn't do confusion.

Her heart skittered again but this time it was nothing to do with excitement—more like dread and fear and trepidation. She *had* to say something.

'I did write to you, you know.'

It sounded pathetic but at least it caught his attention.

'When?' he demanded, his voice hard and tight.

So hard and tight the tiny bit of courage that had prompted Clare to tell him faded, which meant the next words came out all breathless and confused.

'End of January, and again later in the year.

'You wrote to me at the end of January? Wasn't that a bit late, considering it was before Christmas you walked out? I'd definitely moved on by then, physically and emotionally.'

Pain stabbed through Clare's body at the last words, but what was he saying?

'You didn't get *any* letters from me—then or later?'

Glacial green—that's how Oliver's eyes could look…and *were* looking now.

'No.'

He shook his head to emphasise the word and, knowing he would never lie to her, Clare felt a stab of deep resentment—not to mention pain—as she realised he didn't know about her pregnancy. He didn't know he had a daughter, a daughter who would be right there in the flat next door to his come Friday!

She had to tell him!

Easy enough to have the thought but how to do it?

And when, and where?

This was hardly an appropriate time or place and, what's more, he was talking to her again, saying something, although with the wild furore going on her mind it was a struggle to make out the words.

Forcing herself to focus, she realised his conversation was nothing more than the polite inquiries of old acquaintances catching up.

'But a perfusionist? What made you change course? What happened to life on the stage?'

Clare cast an anxious glance behind him, but there was no-one nearby to overhear an almost honest answer.

'Long story short, I moved to Queensland and studied science. I met a perfusionist who used to work with Alex when he was in Melbourne. I learnt more about it and decided it was the dream job as far as I was concerned. I began my studies in Brisbane, then went to Chicago to get more qualifications and experience, and here I am.'

Oliver knew he was staring at her, replacing his mental image of a twenty-five-year-old soap-star Clare with this more mature adult version— more mature, and even more beautiful. And the reaction in his chest was an ectopic heartbeat, nothing more. Ectopic heartbeats happened to some people all the time, and most people some time in their life....

But if he read the signs correctly, she was feeling even more strain at this unexpected meeting than he was.

'Alex was saying we're going to be neighbours.'

Could he really be having this stilted conversation with Clare? Clare who had laughed and loved and thrown herself into life with enormous energy and enthusiasm? Thrown herself into their relationship, making every moment they were together special and intense.

Until the day he'd told her he didn't want a baby and, unable to believe he'd never mentioned this before, unable to even discuss it with him, she'd walked out.…

And he'd let her go, furious at her lack of understanding of his situation—*his* feelings in all of it! How could he have contemplated fatherhood when he didn't know who his own father was, didn't know himself? And how could he have considered marriage when his closest experience of it—his mother's three attempts—had been so disastrous?

He was reminding himself of this justification when Clare spoke again.

'You were saying you've read our landlord's books?'

'There's no need to sound so surprised,' he grumbled, memories of the past bothering him more than he'd thought possible. 'I've time to read these days.'

She smiled at him and he felt his heart miss another beat. Frequent ectopic heartbeats might be indicative of a problem of some kind, his medical brain told him.

'You didn't have time for any relaxation back then,' she said.

Except with you, he thought but didn't say, for there was a barrier between them, like a glass wall through which he could see and hear but not touch. Not that he would touch her, of course. No matter how much his fingers tingled at the thought.

Of course there'd be a barrier between them. It had been ten years; they'd split up. There were issues—wasn't that the word people used these days? So many unresolved issues it was more like a brick rampart than a glass wall between them.

Back to the present!

'My car's illegally parked downstairs. Can I follow you to the flat?'

'You can give me a lift.'

The moment the words were out of her mouth Clare regretted them. She needed to get away from Oliver, not spend more time with him, especially not more time in the privacy a car offered.

She needed time to think things through, to work out how on earth she was going to tell him about Emily.

Not that he deserved to know! He hadn't wanted a child.

The tiny whisper from one corner of her brain was tempting, but she slapped it down. Of course he'd have to know, and now they'd come together, didn't Em deserve to know her father? Hadn't Clare always told Em that one day they'd find him so she could meet him?

But 'one day' in Clare's mind had been when Em was eighteen or so—an adult who would understand the traumatic period of time that had been Clare's pregnancy, not to mention the aftermath of Emily's birth!

She should have directed him to the flat; it was just down the road. But here he was, saying he'd be delighted—ever polite, Oliver

Rankin—and putting out a hand to usher her towards the door.

She moved, just in time to avoid contact with him, but knew that as well as the Emily problem, she had to sort *herself* out, to strengthen her body against the insidious physical weakness just seeing him again had caused. There was too much at stake for her to be distracted by attraction.

'I need to speak to Alex about something, so I'll meet you downstairs. The easiest way is to take the blue exit from the car park. I'll be down there near the gate in five minutes.'

Alex was still at the front of the meeting room, stacking some papers he'd spread out earlier. What excuse could she give? What question could she ask?

Had he noticed her hesitation that he looked up?

'Everything all right, Clare?' he asked. 'Emily settled in at school?'

'Just fine and dandy, and yes, she loves it,' she replied, hovering by her chair while Oliver left the room. But Alex's question had reminded

Clare that Alex and Annie knew Emily, and Rod knew Emily—it wasn't as if you could keep a nine-year-old a secret.

Clare dropped her briefcase, which gave her an excuse to sit down. Knowing she couldn't just sit, she leant down to retrieve the leather case, fiddling with the catches on it while she tried valiantly to regain the poise on which she prided herself, the composure she'd fought so hard to achieve!

'I only know of Angus from his colleagues, but Oliver worked with us earlier this year,' Alex was saying. 'He's a fine surgeon, and if Angus is even half as good as people say he is, we've got a team that you'll discover is every bit as good as the ones you've already worked with. At least, I hope you find it that way.'

Clare smiled at him. He was so *nice*! He and Annie, his wife, had invited her and Emily for dinner the previous Saturday, and seeing their relationship—the obvious love they felt for each other—had left Clare wondering why relationships worked for some people and not for others.

Her body tightened at the memory…

Ached…

Oliver eased his car out of the parking space, thankful he hadn't been clamped. The signs to the blue exit were clear and easy to follow, but it took some manoeuvring to reach it. Clare came hurrying towards him, the movement blurring her image so he saw the beautiful girl who'd first caught his attention—the girl he'd thought was his for ever—running eagerly to meet him.

He couldn't fool himself about ectopic heart-beats any longer; his body was reacting to this bizarre reunion, to her presence, although that could be explained away as well. It was a while since he'd had a relationship with a woman, put off women by the words of his most recent lover who'd informed him he was nothing but an empty shell of a man, with no understanding of love whatsoever.

The woman Clare, not the girl he'd known, climbed into the car and pointed ahead.

'We go through the lights and straight down

that road across from the park. I think most of
the team seem to live along here, though maybe
not the nurses, who'd be local Sydney people.
It's such a pleasant walk to work I haven't considered buying a car yet.'

I, not *we*, Oliver thought, then he had to ask.

'You're on the team list as C. Jackson? You
never married?'

He sensed her withdrawal and knew the glass
wall was very definitely back in place.

'Once, for a very brief time. It was a mistake,'
she said lightly, turning to look out the window
at the houses they were passing. 'We're four
more down, the house with the red door. There's
a common foyer on the ground floor, and stairs
up to a landing. The two flats open off that.
They're fully furnished and very comfortable
but I guess Alex already told you that.'

She might as well have said, Mind your own
business, changing the subject from marriage
to accommodation so swiftly, yet the thought
of Clare with someone else had sent a shaft of
pain through his belly.

Ridiculous, of course; he'd been with other women.

He pulled up outside the house she'd indicated, double-parking as all the marked spaces were already occupied.

'There's a garage around the back. Rod has a vehicle that's been adapted for a wheelchair but there'd be room for another car. Drive on and I'll show you how to get into the lane. Sorry, I didn't think of it earlier.'

Clare knew she was babbling as he followed her directions, but sitting in the close confines of the car with Oliver was even worse than she'd imagined. Somehow she'd been transported back to when they'd met and she'd fallen so helplessly in love—to when *any* time with Oliver was special. Her stupid body was responding to his presence, her physical delight totally uncontrollable no matter how much she tried to overcome it with strong mental warnings.

Even the panic and worry she was feeling over Em did little to dampen her reactions.

'Park here—I'll get the gate. You can ease the

car into the yard while I go in and check with Rod if it's okay to use the garage.'

Finding the gate shut had been a relief. She all but leapt from the vehicle, opening the two sides of the gate, then hurrying to the rear door of Rod's flat.

He was in the small conservatory at the back, his gnarled arthritic fingers pecking furiously at the keyboard of his laptop. She knocked on the glass.

'I hope I haven't ruined your train of thought,' she apologised, 'but Oliver, Dr Rankin, has arrived and has a car. Can he park it beside yours in the garage?'

Rod waved away her apology and wheeled towards her, coming out to meet his new tenant.

'Can't help you with your cases, mate,' he said to Oliver a little later when the car was snug inside the garage and Oliver was heaving two cases from the trunk.

'I can,' Clare found herself offering, but Oliver, being Oliver, refused her offer, carrying them both himself.

'Come through my place,' Rod suggested, and

led the way into his flat, always neat and tidy, the minimum of furniture allowing his chair to move freely through the apartment. He opened his front door, showed them into the foyer and handed Oliver a set of keys.

'Clare will take you up,' he said.

'No papers to sign? No lease agreements?' Oliver asked.

'If you're working for Alex, you're okay,' Rod replied. Then he smiled. 'Actually all the financial details will be in a folder on your kitchen bench. Annie, my daughter, organises all of that for me. Her phone number is there as well as mine, so phone if you need anything or have any questions.'

He then looked from Oliver to Clare before he added, 'Or ask Clare—she's been here a week now, settling in, so she knows her way around.'

He turned from Oliver to Clare and added, 'Have you heard from Emily this week? Does she still think the school's the best in the world?'

Emily! Emily! Emily!

The name hammered in Clare's head, but she *had* to reply.

'She still loves it,' she managed to say, although her vocal cords were so tight it was a wonder the words came out.

'Emily?' Oliver repeated as he followed her up the stairs.

Could she faint? Clare wondered. Faint and topple backwards down the stairs, possibly breaking her neck which right now, extreme though it might be, seemed preferable to answering Oliver's question.

'My daughter,' she managed, forcing the words through even tighter vocal cords, so she sounded shrill, if not hysterical.

'Fancy that! So you got the child you wanted,' Oliver said as they reached the landing. The ice in his voice was visible in his eyes as he looked down at her and added, 'Got the child and dumped the husband once his usefulness was over? Was that how it worked?'

Clare could only stare at him, her mind a chaotic battlefield, one voice yelling at her to tell him right now, another suggesting physical assault, while a third was advocating flight. She steeled herself against them all, looked him in the eyes and, hoping she sounded far more cool and in control than she felt, said, 'You never used to be spiteful, Oliver.'

After which she turned away to unlock her door, and dive into the sanctuary of her flat. Oliver's voice saying her name was the last thing she heard before she shut him out.

She leaned against the door, shaking with the hurt he'd inflicted, trying to breathe deeply, desperate to stem the waves of panic that washed through her mind and body.

Ten deep breaths, wasn't that the rule—no, maybe that was counting to ten before you murdered someone. Well, there was an idea!

Three deep breaths…

Now think rationally!

Monday was as good as done, which meant she had four more days—four days to find a way to tell Oliver Emily was *his* daughter before Em came home and almost inevitably met him in person.

Clare's mind went back into panic mode and breathing deeply didn't seem to help.

Of course she had to tell him. Forget that his reaction just now had been so hateful. He *had* to know!

But the hub of it all was Emily. As far as Clare was concerned, Emily's welfare, her happiness and emotional stability, had to be protected at all costs. Forget how Oliver might feel about Em's mother, forget how Em's parents might feel about each other—or whatever kinds of messes they'd made of their respective lives—at the heart of whatever lay ahead was Emily's well-being.

CHAPTER TWO

OF ALL the impossible things to have happened! Oliver set his cases down in the small foyer and took a look around. Small sitting area, the open plan revealing a dining nook in a bay window and a kitchen behind a high bench at the back.

She had a child.

Stop thinking about Clare; look around your new home.

He could move; Alex had said it would be okay.

No, look around.

Neat, tastefully furnished, all he needed in the way of space. He turned aside, into a reasonably sized bedroom, again a bay window, this one overlooking the front yard and the street and park across the road, while down a small hall he discovered a bathroom and a second bedroom, small, but furnished with a good-size desk as well as a bed, so it was obvious any single tenant would use it as a study.

Or a tenant with a child could use it for the child.

How could he live next door to Clare's child— the child he'd denied her?

A child who wasn't a toddler, if she was at school. Why hadn't he realised just how desperate Clare had been?

Because he'd assumed getting pregnant had been a whim, that's why. Possibly something to make his commitment to her more—

More what?

Binding?

No, she'd known all along he had no intention of marrying and he'd assumed she'd understood that meant no children.

He closed his eyes but her image was once again imprinted in his mind. Not the image from the past, but the image of the new Clare, more heart-stoppingly beautiful than ever.

He swore quietly to himself. Why was he letting her affect him this way? On top of which, the fact that she had a child was none of his business. Where was his self-discipline? Surely he was professional enough that he could treat her as a colleague.

But even as that thought formed in his head another part of his brain was echoing with mocking laughter. As if that's possible, it was saying, when your libido jolts to attention any time she's around. Ectopic heartbeats indeed—be honest, it's lust, mate!

Had it been more than lust the first time? Maybe not love—he wasn't sure what love entailed—but definitely he'd felt a deep affection for her. How could he not when she'd been so beautiful and open and honest?

So loving!

Did she still see their relationship as five wasted years?

No! It was in the past. This was now. And if the child—Emily, Rod had said—was at school, Clare hadn't exactly hung around mourning their break-up.

He gripped his head hard in his hands and

squeezed to stop the mental arguments and to shut out the memories.

He would *not* think about Clare! He would *not* think about the past. He would move on, continue moving on, and if a tiny part of his mind kept questioning whether he'd ever really moved on from Clare emotionally—well, it was such a quiet voice he could ignore it.

She'd moved on, that was for sure. Changed careers, had a child—he doubted she'd ever given him a passing thought.

Until today, of course…

So?

Forget the past!

He took a deep breath, retrieved his cases, carried them through into the bedroom and began unpacking. He had chests with household items awaiting despatch in Melbourne, wanting to settle in and make sure he liked the flat before having them forwarded on, but for now all he needed to unpack were clothes, the one set of sheets he'd brought with him, a couple of towels and books—lots of books, although many more were in the chests. Reading had become his escape, but from what?

It was the first time he'd asked himself that question and now he had to probe further. Was it an escape from thinking too deeply about the sterility of his life? Or an escape from the inner emptiness his old girlfriend had pointed out to him? Or even an escape from feeling anything at all—for anyone…?

He gave a scoffing laugh, and shook off the stupid introspection. Reading was an escape from the intensity of his work, nothing more! And this unfamiliar delving into his psyche was the result of tiredness, having driven through the night to make the meeting this morning, stopping only for a couple of short breaks for safety's sake.

And considering work, rather than the escape from it, he should read up on tomorrow's op. With specialists all over the world, someone was always trying something new—discovering a tidier, or more effective, solution for the myriad problems they encountered.

He found his laptop, opened it on the desk in

the second bedroom and settled down to search the internet. Hours later, stiff and tired, he closed the laptop and went in search of food—or information about food.

He found the folder in the kitchen and leafed through it. There was a selection of takeaway menus at the back of the notes—ha, food! He selected one and made a phone call. He'd eat, then shower, and get a good night's sleep—practical, sensible decision making, that's what was needed here.

A tap at the front door, his flat's front door, made him wonder how people got in—how his pizza would get in. Did the outer door have a bell of some kind, an arrangement whereby it could be opened from upstairs? Had Annie's notes explained? He'd read them again, but first see who was at the door.

Clare!

A very twitchy, uptight-looking Clare for all she smiled politely at him before explaining, 'I thought I should tell you about the doors. On your keys you'll have a bigger shiny silver key, it's for the deadlock on the outside door, but if someone comes to visit you there are bells outside the front door. I've just labelled your bell with your name. You'll hear the ring inside, and the button on that phone thing in the hall—this… Pressing it releases the door lock.'

She'd come in to show him the door-opening mechanism and was so close he could have taken her in his arms right there and then. He could feel her in his arms, feel her curves snug against his body, smell the perfume of her hair in his nostrils. He'd bend his head, just a little, to capture her lips—

He was losing it! Seriously insane! He had to pull himself together, get sorted, all that stuff.

'Thanks,' he managed when she turned to look at him, perhaps puzzled by his wooden stance and lack of response.

'No worries,' she said, then she frowned and looked more closely at him. 'Are you okay? I know it's hardly flattering to tell someone they look terrible, but you look exhausted.'

'Car trouble on the way from Melbourne meant I had to drive through the night. One good night's sleep and I'll be fine.'

Clare turned to leave, uncertain whether to

be glad or sorry. She'd buoyed herself up to tell Oliver about Emily, using the key explanations as an excuse to knock on his door. The plan was she'd casually offer dinner, and they could sit down in a civilised fashion and discuss the situation, though the problem of quite how she'd bring it up still loomed large in her mind.

But seeing how tired Oliver looked and finding out why, it was immediately obvious this wasn't the time to be telling him he had a daughter, especially as he was operating the next morning. What he needed was a good night's sleep, not a bombshell that was likely to rock his world and quite possibly prevent any sleep at all.

Part of her was relieved, but the other part aggravated that the telling would continue to hang over her head.

Then there was dinner—he had to eat… Should she still ask?

'Thanks for explaining about the locks and keys,' he said as she dithered in the doorway, so conscious of his body she wondered if he could feel the tension building in hers. In her mind his hand reached out for her, touched her shoulder, drew her close. She'd sink against him, feeling her body fit itself to his and—

The jangling buzz of the outside bell sounded in his flat, shocking her out of the stupid dream. He smiled as she looked at him, ashamed of her thoughts and puzzled by the intrusion.

'Good thing you labelled my bell,' he added. 'I ordered a pizza for dinner.'

As Oliver pressed the button to release the front door lock, using the phone to tell the delivery person to come on up, Clare scuttled back across the landing, all but diving into the safety of her own flat.

Although as a refuge it was now severely lacking in serenity and peace, given who her neighbour was, and the wayward turns her mind was taking.

Back when he hadn't replied to her letters, she'd put him out of her life, swearing never to think of him again.

But not thinking about him had proven difficult when their child had inherited his green eyes and curving, inviting lips.

* * *

Clare knew she needed a good night's sleep, but how could sleep come when the huge, insurmountable problem of how to tell Oliver was cluttering up her mind and sitting like an elephant on her chest?

Earlier, when she'd gone in with the key excuse, she'd decided just coming out with it would be the best. Oh, by the way, my daughter, Emily, is your child.

But now that seemed impossibly, horribly flippant. She *had* to find some better way to say it.

Oliver, there's something you should know?

No, that wouldn't work. She'd lose courage after the Oliver part and ask about his mother or something equally inane.

Could she begin with self-justification? I did try to contact you; I phoned and wrote, then—

No, she couldn't do that because it would mean explaining about Dad dying and even now thinking of that time still hurt too much for her to talk about it.

Finally, with herculean determination, she

lulled herself to sleep, only to wake before dawn, tired, cranky and so uptight she thought her limbs might snap apart as she moved.

But move she did. Although she'd spent many hours at the hospital the previous week, getting to know the machine she would be operating, now she was anxious to get up to the theatre for one last check.

She showered and dressed, blotting everything from her mind except work, excited yet slightly apprehensive about her first day as part of the team.

Slightly apprehensive?

Understatement of the year, and although she was focusing on work, the other problem set aside, it had to be the thought of working with Oliver that had her twitching like a snake on drugs.

An image of him flashed across her mind— the now-Oliver with silver streaks in the tawny hair, and fine lines at the corners of his green eyes. More lines forming parentheses in his cheeks when he smiled, his lips still as mesmerising as ever, a pale line delineating their shape.

Em's lips!

But it was better to think of Oliver's lips than the problem of Emily right now. Thinking about Emily would put her mother into a panic again and a panicking perfusionist was of no use to anyone.

Unfortunately thinking of Oliver didn't do her much good either. Look at it this way, she told herself. Yes, it was an unbelievable quirk of fate that had brought them together again, but they'd met as colleagues now, nothing more. Two professionals, working in the same team, working to save the lives of tiny babies.

Forget the fact you still feel an attraction to the man!

Forget Emily—well, not Em herself, but the problem she presented right now. Concentrate on work.

In the kitchen, she turned on the simple pod coffee machine that had been her treat to herself when she'd moved to Sydney, and dropped two slices of frozen fruit loaf into the toaster.

Had Oliver found the shops? Did he have food to eat? Coffee?

The temptation to tap on his door and ask him was almost overwhelming, but it was barely six and their official working hours began at eight so it was likely he was still asleep. Besides, the more times she saw him outside of work hours, the more opportunities she would have had to tell him about Emily, and the angrier he'd be when she *did* tell him, that she hadn't told him earlier.

Did that make sense or was her lack of sleep making her stupid?

She sipped her coffee, returning to the mental excuse of not knocking on the door in case he was still sleeping.

An image of a sleeping Oliver popped obligingly into her head—Oliver in boxer shorts, his back bare, lightly tanned, the bones of his spine visible as he curled around his pillow in sleep. An ache started deep inside her, and she left her toast half eaten, the coffee cup still half full, hurrying to the bathroom to clean her teeth, then fleeing her flat which was, she realised, just far too close to Oliver's for her peace of mind. It was the proximity dogging her, reminding her, teasing at her body. If she moved—

But how could she when Alex had been kind enough to arrange the accommodation and she already felt settled here?

Or had done!

Although if she shifted...? *No!* her mind shrieked at her. Of course you have to tell him.

Oliver pushed his bedroom window to open it wider, sure there must be a breeze somewhere in the stillness of the summer morning. Below him the front door clicked shut and Clare strode into view, marching with great speed and determination up the path, then along the street, striding now—exercising or escaping?

But escaping from what? Not him, surely.

He laughed at the thought, a mocking laugh, but didn't leave the window, watching until a slight bend in the road took her out of sight.

Clare!

He showered and dressed, reminding himself

that both of them had changed in the ten years since the split. Now they were mature adults and could meet and treat each other as professional colleagues, nothing more, though the thought of her with a child niggled at him.

For one thing, where was the child now? She hadn't had a child with her and there was no noise coming from next door.

Clare with a child.

Why did that hurt him?

The physical attraction he still felt towards her was probably nothing more than an emotional hangover from the past, some glitch in programming, possibly to do with the Italian revelations. And feeling this strong attraction, it was only natural that he'd been on the brink of taking her in his arms yesterday evening, when the front doorbell had sounded.

Saved by a pizza!

Think of food, not Clare.

Rod's daughter had left some basic groceries in the flat—milk and butter in the fridge, coffee, tea, bread and spreads in the pantry. He'd have to find the supermarket and do some shopping, and until then he could eat at the hospital. In fact, if he left now he could have breakfast there; maybe that's why Clare had left so early.

She wasn't in the little coffee shop in the foyer, nor in the canteen, so he ate a solitary breakfast, then made his way not to the teams' rooms but to the theatre, wanting to refamiliarise himself with the way Alex had it set up.

'Oh!'

Clare was there ahead of him and she must have sensed his presence, for the startled expression burst from her lips before he was fully through the door.

Not that she was unsettled for long, greeting him with a smile—a very professional smile—and a cheery, 'Good morning, Oliver,' for all the world as if they hadn't shared an extremely passionate relationship, albeit ten years ago.

'Do you always begin this early?' he asked, because two could play the calm and controlled game. She smiled again.

'First-night nerves,' she told him. 'I've spent a lot of time here in the past week, but I'm still anxious about the machine, which is stupid as it's exactly the same make of machine as I operated in the States. It's just that—'

She stopped abruptly and he saw a faint colour appear in her cheeks.

'Just that...?' he prompted, hoping professional conversation would halt the disturbances in his body.

'You'll think I'm barmy, but to me the machines have personalities, maybe idiosyncrasies would be a better word, and until I get to know each one personally I won't know what to expect.'

Clare watched him carefully as she explained her unease, and to her surprise, she caught no hint of a smile. In fact, Oliver was nodding as if he understood what she was saying.

'You have so much to think about, with the responsibility for the respiratory and circulatory functions of the lungs and heart. I can understand you wondering if the machine has quirks you need to watch for. You've got the oxygenator, the pumps, the filters, the reservoirs and tubing, so many component parts that can go wrong.'

And now he smiled, sending tremors of re-membered delight through Clare's body, in spite of her determination to remain on strictly pro-fessional terms with him.

'But have things ever gone badly wrong for you? Has there ever been a disaster you couldn't overcome?'

She found herself smiling back at him, profes-sionally, of course.

'Tubes kinking, the membrane oxygenator failing, the machine turning off automatically when a clot or bubble gets into the tubes? I've seen most of the calamities that can happen, and had to cope with a few, but generally the machines, providing they are serviced regu-larly and checked before every operation, work brilliantly.'

Oliver heard the pride in her voice and recog-nised the dedication she had to her profession—speaking of which...

'It still seems a strange choice for someone

who had stars in her eyes and an established career as an actor.'

He saw her shoulders lift in a slight shrug.

'Things happened, Oliver, that changed my goals. I'd done well in science at school, so a switch to that seemed logical.'

Which would have made sense, only her voice had tightened as she spoke, and he sensed a tension in her body. Or was he fooling himself that he was still so attuned to her he could feel her emotion, sense that she'd told maybe not a lie but certainly not the whole truth?

'Then perfusion.'

He shook his head, as much at his own imaginings as at her choice of career. But at least her smile was back—a bright smile now.

'If I'd known how much I would love this job I'd never have bothered with anything else. What amazes me is that there are so many jobs out there that no-one even knows about. I mean, the career adviser at my school didn't mention perfusionist as a career option. In fact, he'd probably never heard of it either. By chance, I met a perfusionist and that was it.'

'So here you are.' Nice, normal conversation; he'd be able to handle this. Always assuming the attraction he still felt towards her wasn't obvious to everyone who came in contact with him when she was around.

She bent her head as she answered, presumably checking some component of the machine, and Oliver found himself studying her, once again imagining he could sense tension in her voice.

'It can't have been easy, handling training and a child.'

It was a throwaway remark, the kind anyone might make, yet he saw her tense. No sensing it this time; he actually saw her stiffen.

Why?

'Mum helped out.'

Obviously that was the only answer he was going to get, so should he keep the conversation going?

Might as well; it was awkward enough as it was without silence extending between them.

'How old is she?'

More silence, then Clare looked up at him.

'She's nine,' she said, before returning to whatever she was doing, fiddling with the machine.

'Nine? As in nine years old?' he muttered as a rage he'd never felt before, not even when his real father had denied him, burnt through his body. 'You're telling me you were so desperate for a child you went from me to him, whoever he was? Or were you already seeing him? Cheating on me? Did he offer marriage? Is that what swayed you? And did he offer before or after you announced you were pregnant, eh?'

Clare had never heard such anger in his voice, yet this was hardly the time to refute his hateful accusations. He was about to operate on a vulnerable infant. He needed to be calm and composed, totally focused on the job, not struggling to comprehend the fact that he had a daughter.

What's more, *she* had to be calm and composed as well! Later she'd get angry. Later she'd tell him....

Right now, she had to defuse the situation somehow.

'It is none of your business what I did or didn't do, Oliver, and right now I really need to get on with this.' She looked up at him again, saw the harsh anger in his face and hated the contempt she read in his eyes. And though her own anger burned at the injustice of his words, she pushed it aside, adding calmly, 'And you probably want to check out the theatre, although didn't Alex say you'd worked with them before?'

For a moment she thought he'd reject the conversational shift, but when he nodded she knew she'd succeeded in tempering the tense emotional atmosphere in the room.

At least for the duration of the operation!

'I *have* worked here before.' Clipped, crisp words, but Clare knew he was turning his focus to work.

'Do we know yet if we have a patient?' she asked, pursuing professional conversation, although he was still unsettling her, prowling around the perimeter of the theatre, distracting her with his presence when she didn't need distraction.

'Last I heard about the TGA Alex listed

yesterday was that he hadn't arrived,' he said, and this time his voice sounded more relaxed—*his* professional self taking over.

'So we wait,' Clare responded, determined to match his tone. 'If Angus is as good at doing a switch of the great arteries as Alex seems to think, it will be exciting to watch him at work. Do you know any more about the patient?'

Oliver shook his head.

'But you still have more contact with them than I do,' she added. 'I usually only get to meet patients when they come into Theatre, although with older children I sometimes do blood collection for autologous blood transfusions should one be necessary. My main contact with newborns is after the op if they go onto ECMO.'

Could she really be having this conversation with Oliver, when the echo of his accusations and the spectre of Emily hung in the room like twin thunder clouds?

'Extracorporeal membrane oxygenation—of course, you're in charge of those machines as well.'

'Terrible necessities,' Clare said. 'Some

babies need them post-op but they can do so much damage to the organs if we're not really careful.'

She continued on about the problems the machine could cause, but Oliver had stopped listening to the actual words, hearing instead the confidence and professionalism in her voice, noticing the tension had lessened.

Maybe it had never been there. Maybe he'd imagined it!

Or maybe she was as good as he was at compartmentalising her life. It had taken him a mammoth effort, a few minutes ago, to block out the implications of the age of Clare's child, but he'd done it, because the baby they were about to treat had to be his sole focus for the next few hours.

His pager buzzed against his belt and he glanced at the message.

'Looks like it's all systems go,' he said, and heard Clare's pager buzz at the same time.

'Good luck,' she said, smiling now, no hiding the excitement in her eyes. She was rising to the challenge that lay ahead, totally professional, the adrenaline rush in her veins lighting her up from within.

So why was he seeing black shadows hovering over her—the shadow of another man, another man's child? Why was totally inappropriate anger festering inside him?

'Good luck yourself,' he said, blotting the dark clouds from his mind, repelling the anger from his body. In eighteen years of professional life he'd never allowed his work self to be distracted by outside issues and he wasn't about to start now.

And the tension he was feeling at the base of his spine was because he was working with a new team, nothing else.

Other members of the team breezed in, inconsequential chat filling the air as people went about their allotted tasks while the atmosphere in the theatre seemed to tighten in expectation of the operation that lay ahead.

'You're opening?' the circulating nurse asked Oliver.

In work mode now, totally focused, he nodded, then examined the instruments she'd laid out on a trolley. It would be his job to open the tiny chest, cutting through skin and the rib cage, using retractors to hold the ribs open and allow a clear field for operating.

'Do you need a small suture?' the nurse asked, and Oliver thought about what lay ahead. As he separated out the pericardium—the fine sheath of protective tissue that surrounded the heart—he would often take a tiny piece of it, and secure it to a spot in the baby's chest, in case the surgeon needed it later to repair a hole in one of the interior walls of the heart.

The baby!

It seemed impersonal to think of him or her that way, but every one of them was very real to Oliver and every one he was involved in saving was special, even though his contact with them, at this stage, was minimal.

The baby!

His mind wavered for a moment—Clare's baby, the one he hadn't wanted, intruding—but only for a millisecond.

'Leave a suture there—I'll ask Angus when he comes in. I know from working with Alex that he always likes to have a piece of tissue in reserve.'

The nurse slipped the threaded needle onto the tray, while Oliver checked he had all he needed, shifting a couple of instruments into an order he was used to, in spite of the fact he would rarely pick up an instrument himself.

'Okay, folks, we have a baby to save.'

Kate Armstrong, the anaesthetist, erupted into the room, nodding and smiling at everyone, then stopping beside Clare to discuss drugs and dosages. Oliver studied the two women—Clare, tall and straight, Kate smaller, but with so much animation in her face she seemed more of a presence. Her vibrant red hair was wrapped in a scarf, but its energy seemed to escape so she had an aura of liveliness about her.

Yet it was Clare who drew his eyes, although he didn't know this Clare at all....

He likes her. The thought came to Clare as she watched Oliver looking at Kate, and it niggled in her chest in a way it had no right to niggle, especially after the angry, hateful accusations he'd thrown at her earlier.

No, apart from whatever relationship he developed with Em, Oliver was no longer her concern. He could like whomever he cared to like, though for a moment Clare wished she had the same kind of lively personality Kate had—a personality that attracted men. Instead, she had a face and figure—outward things—that drew their attention.

The arrival of their patient put an end to any extraneous thoughts. As the nurses set the patient up for surgery, and Oliver, as the first assistant, began the simple part of the operation, Clare checked and rechecked her machine, watching the monitors, talking quietly to Kate from time to time, discussing the blood values they were getting.

But she watched Oliver as well, noticing how gently his hands touched the infant, how carefully he cut and opened up the little chest. She smiled to herself, remembering how much he'd loved his paediatric patients, back when they were together, how special he had thought each and every one of them.

Was that why she'd been so stunned when

he'd said he didn't want children? Although they'd never discussed the subject until she brought it up that fateful time, she'd always assumed, somewhere down the track, Oliver, loving children as he did, would want children of his own.

CHAPTER THREE

ANGUS arrived and the operation proceeded smoothly, Clare relieved for the baby's sake when it was successfully completed. But her job wasn't done, not with the baby still on a support system. She and Kate accompanied him to the small recovery room off the main cardiac PICU, Clare concerned about her first patient as part of this elite team, while Kate explained that she always wanted to see her patients come out of the anaesthetic. When Kate left for a moment to check something on the ward, Clare looked down at the little boy with tubes and monitor leads practically obliterating his small body.

'They're so vulnerable,' she whispered to herself. 'But so valiant.'

'They are indeed! We do terrible things to their bodies and they come out of it so well.'

She looked up at his voice, still startled by

it, still unnerved by the coincidence of Oliver being in the same team.

Unnerved, unsettled and, remembering his remarks in Theatre earlier, angry.

Definitely angry.

Very angry.

But when Angus came in to check on the patient, Oliver left.

'Look, there's no point in all three of us being here,' Kate said, soon after. She waved her hand towards Clare and Angus. 'Why don't you two grab a coffee break—in fact, it's past lunchtime. The canteen is good, and cheaper than the coffee shop on the ground floor. You know where to go?'

Why was Kate so keen to send them away?

Not that it mattered. Kate was right that they did not all need to be there. It was a very small room. Angus was apparently open to the suggestion, for he was already holding the door for Clare.

But it was Oliver she *should* be talking to. As hateful as his words had been earlier, she *had* to tell him! Not that she could tell him in a hospital canteen...

Although where *could* she tell him?

Was there an optimal place for telling a man he had a nine-year-old daughter?

'Yes, I'm glad that first one's over,' she said to Angus in reply to his polite conversation about the op. But as they reached the canteen she knew she had to stop asking herself impossible questions about the Oliver situation and toss the conversational ball back to Angus.

'I'm using the same machine, but did you find the set-up much different to the way you worked in the States?'

After that it was easy, normal conversation about work, but although Angus was a very good-looking man with dark hair and eyes and a soft Scottish accent that should be sending ripples up her spine, neither looking at nor listening to him did anything to her.

He was a nice man, she decided, a little reserved and without the magnetism that drew her to Oliver, but very nice all the same.

Magnetism?

Oliver?

Wasn't her reaction to him—the physical attraction thing—just a hangover from the past?

And how could she even think of being attracted to a man who thought so little of her?

There were no ripples up her spine from Angus because she was totally spineless!

'I really should go back,' she said as, coffee finished, the conversation dried up. She needed to escape, preferably to a dark cave where she could hide out while she sorted out her life.

Or at least until she worked out how to tell Oliver her child was also his.

A week ago, life had seemed so simple, been such an adventure. She and Em coming back to Australia, setting up house, just the two of them, for the first time. Now everything had erupted into chaos.

'Are you all right?' Angus asked, and Clare realised she'd been twisting her table napkin so tightly it had curled into something that looked very like a miniature noose.

'Nervous about the baby,' she said, hoping her voice wouldn't reveal her lie.

'So, let's check on him together,' Angus said.

Together was good. She wouldn't be on her own if they ran into Oliver.

Which they didn't, although the baby—now named Bob—had his parents with him at the moment, so Clare contented herself with sitting by the nurse on duty at his monitor, watching the information feeding out from all the paraphernalia attached to him.

Oliver didn't reappear, which was both a relief and a cause of anxiety. She *had* to talk to him!

But just imagining that conversation filled her with such apprehension she found herself literally shaking. Bob was doing well and she had no excuse to hang around so she made her way to the team tea room, thinking another strong coffee might settle her nerves and, once they were settled, surely her brain would start working again.

No, that was the coward's way out. Oliver wasn't in the PICU, but he'd have an office somewhere in the unit rooms. On his first full day of work, he wouldn't be seeing patients but he was likely to be in his office, reviewing files of children he would be seeing later in the week, patients he'd be taking over from the specialist who'd left the team.

Bypassing the tea room, and the meeting room next to it, Clare made her way down the corridor to where Becky, the unit secretary, had her office.

Was fate telling Clare not to do this now because Becky was absent from her desk?

Nonsense, the names are on the doors. You've passed Alex's and Angus's offices; Oliver's is probably next. It wasn't but it *was* further down the corridor. Dr Oliver Rankin!

Before she could lose her nerve as she had last night, Clare knocked and heard Oliver's voice bid her enter.

He was sitting at a wide desk, files stacked in neat piles all over it. The light from the window behind him threw his face into shadow, making any expression impossible to read, but just seeing him brought back the angry accusations he'd made earlier and the injustice of them made her own anger rise.

She was about to let fly—to just come out with the fact that Emily was *his* daughter— when he disarmed her with a smile.

And an apology!

'I had no right to speak to you as I did earlier,' he said, standing and coming around the desk to where three easychairs were set up with a small coffee table in the middle.

Now she could see his face, but although she studied it closely, she couldn't read the motive behind the words.

Should she accept them at face value?

When he had her so churned up she felt she might be physically sick at any moment?

No way!

'No, you had no right at all, Oliver,' she said, quelling the nausea that clutched at her stomach. 'But I haven't come to talk about that—well, not about what you said. But yes, about Emily, my daughter—our daughter.'

The words were out before she realised it, and

now hung in the air between them like graffiti letters on a big balloon.

'*Our* daughter?'

Such steely contempt in his words and his eyes that Clare shivered, but Oliver had put her down once today; he wasn't going to do it again!

'Yes, *our* daughter,' she snapped. 'What with Christmas and being distraught over our break-up I didn't realise I was pregnant until late January, and then I tried to contact you but you'd left the apartment and your mobile number and email address had changed, and when I called the hospital they said you'd left but wouldn't tell me where you'd gone. I phoned your mother but she wouldn't speak to me, so I wrote to you at your mother's address and, now I've met up with you again, I realise you must never have got the letters, although at the time I did wonder if you hated me so much you didn't care about your child.'

The words came tumbling out so quickly Clare realised she must have practised them more often than she'd thought. Maybe in the dream state before she went to sleep some nights, when memories of Oliver had crept like whispers into her heart.

But now they *were* out she slumped into a chair, as if getting rid of them had stolen her strength.

Oliver looked at her, elbows on her knees, bent head held in her hands, an image that could be called despair.

Obviously he was thinking of how Clare looked because he couldn't take in the enormity of what she'd told him, and thinking about something else was far preferable to trying to make sense of the blurted-out confession.

He had a child?

Her child was his?

A girl called Emily?

It was a nice name.

He groaned and took a turn around the room, unable to believe he'd had such an irrelevant thought at a moment of such magnitude in his life.

'You wrote to me? Where?'

This wasn't quite the issue either, but anger

had begun to burn deep inside him and he had to get it out.

'At the apartment and your mother's house. I even wrote care of the hospital but it was returned. I wrote when I couldn't contact you by phone or email, and I wrote again when Emily was born.'

Now some of his anger found a new target—oh, there was still plenty for Clare but right now it focused on his mother.

'She must have destroyed the letters,' he said, speaking to himself, hearing the tightness of his fury in his voice. 'But you could have phoned her again, told her about the baby—'

'Would she have passed on the information if she wasn't passing on the letters? Maybe she already knew, maybe she'd read them before destroying them. She never considered me good enough for her son, so would she want a grandchild if I was the mother?'

Clare looked at him and shook her head, adding in an exhausted voice, 'Anyway, it's all irrelevant now. You didn't know. I thought you did and I hated that you didn't care. The point is that Em's missed nine years of knowing her father, although I've talked to her about you, and now you—well, we, I suppose—have to decide where to go from here. Given that she's just started at a new school and is boarding for the first time, I don't want her upset.'

'Boarding? You've sent a nine-year-old to boarding school? Didn't I tell you what I thought of parents who dumped their kids in boarding schools? Don't you remember me telling you how much I hated it?'

Once again Oliver was aware this was a side issue, but it was all he could manage as his mind was still struggling to accept he was a father. Clare was standing up again now, and she touched his arm as she explained.

'She's a weekly boarder, so she comes home every Friday and leaves again on Sunday evening. Up until this year, Mum lived with us and looked after her when I was studying or at work, but I knew it was time Mum had a break—she's got other grandchildren to fuss over. And Em's mad for horses so this school is ideal as they can take riding lessons, and have horse camps during the holidays. My cousin Caitlin is a senior at the school and she's keeping an eye on Em as well.'

'Em!'

The name came out as a roar of pain or rage. Oliver wasn't sure which it might have been; he only knew he had to move, to get away from Clare before he exploded and did or said something he might regret. He went back behind his desk, staring at the neat stacks of files he'd made on it, wishing his mind was as well ordered, instead of the churning, swirling mess boiling around inside his head.

He had a child, a daughter—Emily...Em!

Clare moved towards the desk, though warily, he thought, stopping out of touching distance, her arms wrapped around her chest as though she was cold, or maybe fearful.

'I hated my name being shortened when I was at school,' he snapped, and she stared at him as if she couldn't fathom what he'd said, although more likely she was puzzled as to why he'd said it.

Join the club!

'Oliver,' she said quietly, 'I know I've dumped a bombshell on you and you'll need time to think about it, but we don't have to talk about it any more right now.'

She reached out her hand as if to touch him across the table, to bridge the gulf that had widened between them, but anger still held sway within him and he turned away from the proffered hand, staring blindly out the window.

She *could* have found him!

She'd *chosen* not to!

And there was more to this than she was telling—the timing was just *too* suspicious.

He swung to face her.

'*You knew you were pregnant*—that's why you left! All that talk of it being a good time for you to take a break from your career, about how easy it would be to write you out of the show by sending you on an overseas holiday, then you could come back in later. You had it all worked out! When did you stop taking the pill? How far back had you planned this? Before Owen told me he wasn't my father, or did you do it after that, knowing how I felt?'

The words were like a fist to Clare's stomach and she flinched away from him.

But not for long!

'It was not planned,' she said, standing very upright and speaking with cold deliberation. 'Nor did I know when we parted. There is just no way I would have kept something like that from you. I thought you knew me well enough to realise that.'

No response, while his face, with the setting sun behind it, might have been carved in granite so little did it reveal.

'Anyway,' she continued valiantly, though her heart was pumping wildly and her body shaking with the tension, 'this is not about the past, and what did or didn't happen, but about Emily and whether or not you want to be part of her life as her father.'

'And you expect me to decide that now?'

The growled words seemed to Clare to contain a hint of menace, and once again her body flinched, but she stood her ground.

'No, Oliver. I know you need time to assimilate this, and to consider things, but you must realise I had to tell you.'

Oliver stared at her for a moment longer, then turned away again.

Had she been pregnant?

Surely it was too big a coincidence that she'd left him because he didn't want children, *then* discovered she was pregnant! Far too big a coincidence!

And as for not being able to contact him. She *could* have found him.

His anger built again, then faltered as a cool voice whispered through the random thoughts cartwheeling through his head.

She thought she had.

Maybe.

He wasn't ready to concede that yet.

'Oliver!'

He turned to face her again, taking in her upright posture, her head held high, challenge in every line of her body.

'This is not the time for recrimination,' she said, voice cool, although he thought he caught a slight waver in it. 'You can think what you like about me but what you have to decide is how much involvement you want to have with Emily, then we have to work out how and when to tell her. She has to come first in all of this. We're adults and we're supposed to be able to handle flak in our lives—she's a child and it's our duty to protect her.'

Oliver bit back the 'you're her mother, you tell her' response that leapt to his lips. Emotional reactions were *not* appropriate right now. Clare was right. They had to put the child first. But for possibly the first time in his life, his usually clear and analytical brain had gone AWOL. He couldn't string two thoughts together, let alone form a plan for introducing a nine-year-old to her father.

And did he want to be a father? It was all very well deciding in principle that he didn't want a child, but now he knew one existed, how was he going to handle it?

By rejecting her as first Owen and then his birth father had done to him?

Totally unacceptable.

Unthinkable.

Anger burned, directed once again, possibly unfairly, at Clare for putting him in this position, but before he could find words to release it, she was speaking again.

'Perhaps if you could get to know her as a person first, then we do the father thing later,' she suggested.

'You mean do things with the two of you at weekends, then in a few weeks, if she doesn't take against me for some reason, announce that I'm her father?'

Boy, was that ever a legitimate reason for anger release!

Clare felt her shoulders slump again as this new wave of Oliver's attack washed over her. She sat down again, the better to absorb it.

Of course they couldn't do that to Em.

'I'll have to tell her straightaway—explain you never got my letters, and so you didn't know about her. She knows your name anyway. I've talked about you—'

'And told her what?' Oliver demanded, fury still reverberating in his voice. 'That her father didn't care enough to want her? That I didn't want a child at all?'

His accusations were so unjust Clare couldn't help herself. She glared at him across the desk, although she knew anger only bred more anger and that arguing was futile.

'Well, did you? At least be honest, Oliver. We split up because a child was the last thing you wanted—then or ever. And you had logical reasons to back up your stance—your own childhood, not knowing who your father was, not wanting to pass on an uncertain heritage to a child. You were definite enough!'

But even through her anger she could still feel the manifestations of attraction, all the physical magnetism that Oliver had always exerted over her. And feeling them, looking at him, seeing his pale, tight face, she wanted nothing more than to go to him and put her arms around him, to comfort him as he grappled with this momentous, life-altering news.

She was pathetic.

After the way he'd behaved, *she* wanted to comfort *him*.

'How much does she know about me?'

The physical reactions lessened at the abrupt question, but at least it was something Clare could answer honestly.

'Quite a lot. She knows you're a doctor, a paediatrician, and from when she was quite young she decided off her own bat that the reason you weren't around like some other kids' fathers was because you were too busy looking after sick babies.'

Oliver felt a growl beginning deep down in his throat, but he held it there, breathing deeply, knowing getting angry again wouldn't help anything. Clare's words had somehow made his daughter come to life, and though his anger at Clare still simmered deep inside him, a different churning had begun. He'd been cheated out of nine years of his daughter's life and was now expected to step into a fatherhood he hadn't wanted.

With an effort of iron will, he forced himself to calm down, to think rationally.

He mentally repeated what Clare had told

him, and realised it might help them sort the 'telling Emily' problem out.

'I've been overseas—so have you—so obviously we couldn't have been looking after the same sick babies up until now. But surely if she knows about me, can't you just tell her we've met up again? Exciting news—her father's working in the same place as you are!'

He got that far before apprehension swamped him, and he stood from behind the desk to pace again.

'*Would* it be exciting news for her?'

'It would be the ultimate in exciting news for her,' Clare said, so softly he had difficulty making out the words.

'The problem is,' she continued, 'where do we go after the excitement. I can't give her a father who really doesn't want to be a father, one who's not willing to go the whole way. That doesn't just mean going to parent-teacher meetings and taking her to the zoo, but guiding her path through life, teaching her right and wrong, disciplining her when necessary and helping her cope with things like bullying, and jealousy, and teachers she thinks are mean to her at school.'

She paused, then while Oliver was still trying to take in all she'd said, she added, 'You'd have to be a dad.'

How could he be a dad?

He, who'd never really known his father—well, the father he'd thought was his?

Owen had been cold, reserved and distant. Because Oliver wasn't his blood son? Perhaps, but even as a stepfather he hadn't been much of a model for Oliver to follow, and the men who'd come into his mother's life after Owen hadn't bothered to pretend to be interested in their stepson.

'I'll leave you to think about it,' Clare said, standing again, but Oliver was so lost in his own thoughts he barely heard her, simply nodding, although he realised the conversation was far from over.

Escaping from Oliver's office had been relatively easy, but escaping her thoughts and turbulent emotions were an entirely different matter.

Except that she still had work, and turning her mind to work would at least block out any thoughts of Oliver and where they stood in regard to Emily.

She made her way to the PICU where Bob was now installed. At least she didn't have to worry about how he looked. He lay in his crib, all pink and contented, totally beautiful if you ignored the dressings and tubes and monitor leads. Not wanting to intrude as both his parents were by his side, Clare checked the machine was working smoothly, that all the settings were correct, then slipped away, stopping by the outside monitors, where she watched the screens which were confirming he was doing well.

'I'm leaving the hospital now,' she told the nurse who was watching Bob's screens, 'but I'll have my pager, so if there's any change don't hesitate to contact me.'

'You and all the rest of the team,' the woman said, smiling at Clare and pointing to the list of numbers by the monitors. 'This little guy has captured a lot of hearts in a short space of time.'

'They all capture mine,' Clare admitted. 'So small and so resolute, the way they come through the terrible stresses we put on their little bodies. Every one of them is a miracle.'

'Aren't all babies miracles, especially for their parents?' the nurse asked, and Clare nodded her agreement.

Think of Bob, she told herself as she left the hospital. Think of the part you play in saving the lives of babies like him. Think positive, woman! You can handle this situation. Em will handle it as well. Okay, so it might be a bit awkward at first, but eventually the three of them should be able to find a way to fit Oliver into Em's life, and Em into his, without too much disruption.

When Clare left his office, Oliver replayed in his mind the list of things she'd said he'd have to do—a very small part of dadhood, he imagined—but though theoretically they all seemed doable, the idea of someone bullying his daughter at school filled him with a white-hot rage.

Clare would have to handle things like that, but what about all the other stuff he heard parents discussing, like how much television their children should watch, and the perils of the internet.

He slumped down into his chair, banged his head against the desk and groaned.

Being a father in name only wasn't an option—Clare had made that abundantly clear—but could he take on the task that was becoming more mountainous every time he thought about it, new worries like adolescence and dating sneaking into his head?

Damn the woman! Surely it would have been easier if they'd been together all the time, and he'd have had the opportunity to grow into the job.

Feeling justifiably aggrieved now, he stacked the files into one pile. He'd have to read them some other time, some time when he might manage to take in what was in them. For now he had to think, had to talk some more to Clare, had to work out just where in his life he could fit a daughter.

Or where his daughter might fit him in!

Clare would have to help him. Had she gone

home? He glanced at his watch and realised it was late enough for her to have left the hospital, but with baby Bob Stamford on ECMO would she be on duty?

She wasn't in the PICU, although according to the Stamfords, she'd just left. He set off for his flat, striding down the road, feeling hard done by again. How could he possibly be a dad? He found the source of his aggravation sitting on the front fence.

'Most fathers learn on the job,' he told her without any lead-in conversation at all, 'so it's easier than having it dumped on them like this.'

She studied him for a moment, then half smiled.

'At least be honest with yourself, Oliver,' she said. 'How much learning time would you have had? Had we still been together, how often would you have been home to bathe Emily, or change a nappy, or play with her, or read her a bedtime story? You're thinking of you now, all qualified, but back then?'

She was right but no way would he admit

it, although a change of subject might be in order.

'What are you doing sitting out here?'

It was a full smile this time, though her flushed face suggested it was hiding embarrassment.

'Changing the subject? I forgot my keys. I kind of rushed away and must have left them in my locker at the hospital. Rod's not home, so I was hoping you'd eventually return and open the front door.'

'And your flat? How do you propose to get into that?'

The smile became more natural.

'I keep a key above the door. I've always had a key hidden somewhere outside in case I lost mine, or Em lost hers and something happened and she needed to get in. Rod's usually home downstairs, but she knows if he's not home Annie's got a key for the outside door, so all bases are covered.'

A horror he'd never felt before crept into Oliver's bones, turning the marrow to ice.

'She's nine years old,' he said, restraining the yell to a muted roar. 'Why on earth would she ever be out on her own and need a key to get back in? What kind of a mother are you, to be letting a nine-year-old roam the city on her own?'

Feeling incredibly weary, and sorry she'd ever started the Emily conversation, Clare stood.

'For your information she doesn't roam the city on her own, but things happen. I just believe she must always know how to get into her own home, in case something *were* to happen when she *might* find herself alone and need the refuge of her home. She also, if you want to know, has a mobile phone and a cab charge card. I realise it's so unlikely it's stupid to even talk about, but what if she ran away from school? You did several times, I remember you telling me. What if she has your running-away-from-school gene?'

She walked towards the door, then realised the man with the key was still standing where she'd left him by the fence.

'Do you have to think ahead that much?' he demanded. 'All the time? Do you have to imagine every possible eventuality and plan for them? Is that what parenting is all about?'

Clare walked back and stood beside him.

'You can never imagine every eventuality, believe me, but you can plan for the ones you do imagine—that way you sleep better at night. Not well, mind you, because there are always bits of child worry buzzing about in your brain, but better.'

She touched his arm to draw him towards the door, feeling exhausted by the tension and emotion of the day, and wanting nothing more than to have a hot shower and collapse into her bed.

He walked with her towards the porch, obviously thinking over what she'd said. Finally he unlocked the front door, opened it and stood back for her to enter first. The sensor light came on and she climbed the steps, every one an effort, but when she reached above her lintel for her key and opened the door, he stopped her with a hand on her shoulder.

'You do realise we'll have to get married,' he said.

CHAPTER FOUR

CLARE stalled in the doorway.

Surely Oliver couldn't have said what she thought he'd said!

Dismissing it as some kind of hallucinatory madness, she took another step into the sanctuary of her flat, but that didn't stop her hearing his next words.

'It's the only sensible thing to do—and the best thing for Emily, you must admit.'

Now she had to acknowledge the words were real. She spun towards him.

'Are you mad? Get married? What on earth put such an absurd idea into your head?'

He'd followed her into her flat, for now he was there, right in front of her, his body sending out those weakening subliminal messages, her own body, lacking any steel at all, responding.

'Everything you read tells you that children

brought up by two parents are better adjusted than those from single-parent families.'

'That's rubbish and you know it. For as many articles you find saying that, there are just as many to refute it. As if a child isn't better off with one happy, well-adjusted parent than with two who are at war all the time.'

'But would we be at war?' he asked, so softly she wondered if she'd imagined the words. But when he leant towards her and added, '*All* the time?' she knew exactly where the argument was going. The physical attraction she'd been trying to deny since he'd come back into her life hadn't been all one way, and now Oliver was going to use it against her.

She could have moved, should have moved, but her legs refused to obey the instructions from her brain. Perhaps because they'd been very weak instructions, while the one from her brain to her lips—don't kiss him back—was positively pathetic.

His mouth claimed hers, capturing her lips and defeating any feeble resolve she might have had, for kissing Oliver was so mind-blowing she could only feel, and touch, and kiss him back.

Feel.

Surely there was a better word to describe the wave of languorous warmth the kiss brought with it, to describe the way her body grew heavy with excitement, the way her nipples peaked and tingled as they brushed against his chest. This wasn't feeling; this was bliss. It was wonderment and ecstasy and a hunger so deep and haunting she began to ache with it.

She wanted more; she wanted all of him, her body splayed across his now, he her sole support. The kiss had left her lips, his mouth moving to her temple, then her ear, her skin shivering beneath his attentions. Then those questing lips found her neck, the hollow where the heavy thunder of her pulse would be a dead giveaway of her arousal.

Clare knew she should break away, or at the very least stop responding to his kisses, but it was as if ten years had never been—no, that was wrong. It was the gap of ten years, that huge, insurmountable gap, that made the kisses so mind-blowingly intense. Heat raced through her body, not languid warmth now but something fierce and searing, burning away memories and scars she'd thought would stay for ever.

Oliver's body hummed with excitement, stirring, hardening, seriously hungering for the woman in his arms, his erection hard against her belly. His hand skimmed her breasts, felt the peaked nipples that told of her excitement, then he caught one lightly in his fingers and—

She was gone, pushing away from him, shuddering, shivering, pale as milk. He reached out for her but she spun away.

'Please go, Oliver!'

The words were shaky, strangled, but he heard pain and terror in them, so crystal clear he backed away without a second thought, shutting her door behind him.

But after unlocking his own door, he didn't go inside. He remained on the landing, listening, worried now that there was something seriously wrong. His mind was totally occupied by Clare, Emily pushed into the background, although he knew he'd have to give *that* matter more thought.

And soon!

For now, he stood in his hallway, the door still open, wondering about Clare, puzzling over her extreme reaction.

Puzzling wouldn't help, especially as the reasons that leapt to mind were very discomforting.

He'd think about Emily instead, but his mind wouldn't move past the whiteness of Clare's face and the horror in her dark eyes as she'd backed away from him.

Was she okay?

Of course she was. She was probably in bed by now.

Bed.

As he'd kissed her, ideas of bed had inevitably filtered into his mind, certain that the kisses would lead—if not tonight, but one night soon—to them resuming their physical relationship.

Until she'd flinched away…

It wasn't frustration gnawing at him now, preventing him from even considering his major problem—he had a daughter. It was that flinch—Clare's reaction.

He'd hurt her, he knew that, back when they'd parted. Then, not hearing from him and assuming he'd ignored her letters about her pregnancy would have hurt her even more.

But that had been emotional hurt. Could it extend to the physical, to the extent that she'd all but fainted when he'd touched her breast?

He shook his head.

There was no way he could guess the answers to his questions and he suspected he was thinking of Clare to stop himself thinking of his daughter—of Emily. But how could he think about a child he didn't know? Where did he start?

Feeling anger rise again, he moved, striding into the living room and slumping down into one of the surprisingly comfortable armchairs. Rod Talbot knew his furniture. And why was he thinking about Rod Talbot and furniture? Again the answer was Emily.

Perhaps if he didn't think at all, simply went about his business as if nothing had happened, his subconscious could chivvy away at the problem and maybe come up with some answers for him. Answers to questions like how do you get to know a nine-year-old? How do you even talk to a nine-year-old?

No, he knew how to do that—he'd had patients who'd been nine. He *could* talk to children, even if all the practice he'd had had been with patients, not daughters.

A daughter!

What did she look like?

Why hadn't he asked Clare?

He glanced towards his still-open front door, but there was no light visible beneath her door, and no sounds coming from her flat.

He could wake her up and ask her, ask to see a photo—surely he deserved that much!

Pride restrained him.

Pride and the memory of her milk-white face...

He took himself to bed, only to find images of small girls flocking through his head—small girls with dark eyes and hair, pigtails maybe, toothy smiles. Did she need braces, was she tall or short? He gave an anguished moan and sat up. If he wasn't going to sleep he could do some work. Alex had mentioned a new case coming in, an infant with Down syndrome and the added complication of an atrioventricular septal defect.

Because AVSDs were more common in children with Down syndrome, most of them had an echocardiogram soon after birth, even if no heart murmur was audible. Oliver opened his computer, doing a search through restricted medical sites for the latest information on the operation and its success rate. He was pleased to see it was now listed at ninety-seven percent success rate, though some patients, less than ten percent, had to return to Theatre later in their life for further surgery due to a leaky mitral valve.

Reminding himself of the procedure was a good idea, for now he could go to bed and run through it in his head—every intricate step—until sleep claimed him.

Slumped on the side of the bath, Clare held her head in her hands and tried to think, but her

brain was exhausted by all the emotional upheaval of the evening and her body was drained
of all energy.

How could she have reacted like that? What
must Oliver have thought? Why hadn't she
known that this might happen?

Tears streamed down her face—she, who
thought she'd emptied out all the tears provided
for her lifetime years ago!

She wrapped her arms around her body, shivering and shaking, ashamed that the nightmare
of the past should have come back to haunt her
at that moment, and in that way. And what
must Oliver have thought of her behaviour, one
moment responding to his kisses with all the
fervour of a lover and the next shrinking, fleeing from him.

Mentally unbalanced—that's what he'd
think, and from there it was only a small step
to wondering if she was a fit mother for his
daughter.

No! Don't make things worse. You can handle
this.

She nodded her response to the voice in her

head. She'd have a shower and go to bed and not think about anything but sleep.

Well, sleep and Emily. Forget the past and think of the future. Go forward, that's what they both had to do. They had three days to work things out. Em had phoned at daybreak this morning to tell her there was a party of some kind at the boarding school—year-twelve students leaving?—so she wouldn't be coming home until Saturday morning and could Mum please collect her at nine.

Of course Mum could, Clare had assured her, and although normally she'd have felt a quick stab of depression at missing out on another night of her daughter's company, with the advent of Oliver into her life again, the extra night had seemed like a blessing.

Oliver!

How could he think getting married would solve anything?

Although maybe he'd changed his mind about that idea after she'd pushed away from him.

Not that she could think of marrying Oliver, not now she knew how she'd react to his touch.

He'd expect them to have a sexual relationship—why wouldn't he expect it when he knew the attraction was still so strong between them?—but it would be impossible.

Memories, images, flashed across her mind, things she thought shut away forever tumbling through her head, making her feel so dizzy she had to sit again, breathing deeply to calm herself as she shoved the memories back where they belonged—back into the past.

She stripped off her clothes, then did something she rarely did—looked at her naked body in the mirror. The scars on her breasts were faint now, probably more in her mind than on her skin, but as she looked at them shame flooded through her.

No, she couldn't marry Oliver!

Turning away from the tormenting image, she stepped under the shower, hoping having the water run hot and hard would wash away the ache of regret that grew inside her.

Of *course* she couldn't marry Oliver.

But wouldn't it be the best solution for Emily?

A platonic marriage?

A likely idea! Maybe if she hadn't kissed him, hadn't responded to his kisses like some sex-starved maniac, she could sell the platonic idea, but now it was too late.

Too late to even dream of such a thing, although later, as she lay in bed, she did dream of it, even feeling his hands on her body, exciting it as only Oliver could, then the dream turned to a nightmare, Oliver looking at her and backing away, repulsed by scars that had grown all over her body—scars that even in the dream she knew she didn't have.

Damaged goods!

Did he say the words in the dream, or had she heard them as an echo in her head? Either way she woke in the early hours of the morning to find her pillow wet with tears.

She had to sleep. It was nothing but a bad dream. They'd work things out, she and Oliver, without having to get married. Getting married was just another dream, a different kind of dream—a foolish daydream that he'd awoken with his words.

Years of practice had taught her how to turn off her churning thoughts before she went to sleep, but tonight none of her strategies worked, until she thought of Emily, and remembered the excitement in her daughter's voice this morning, the delight that she, a newcomer, had been included in the party.

Em's joy was proof that being the child of a single-parent household hadn't done her any irrevocable harm thus far. And thinking of Emily, happy and secure, helped Clare block out all the horrors the night had stirred up, and she was able to drift back to sleep.

Waking up, however, was a different matter. Happy and secure Emily might be, but when told she was about to meet her father...? How was she going to react to that? Clare had been so uptight about telling Oliver, she'd given little thought to the problem of how to introduce Emily to her father.

Unrefreshed from the restless night's sleep and still feeling the effects of the stress-ridden previous twenty-four hours, Clare made her way to work. She was in Theatre with Alex today and hopefully Oliver would still be working with Angus, but she'd no sooner arrived in Theatre to have a chat to her machine, than Oliver appeared.

'I'd like a photo if you've got one.'

Great opening! Although she should be thankful he was speaking to her at all, after her behaviour the previous evening. She faced him without flinching, outwardly at least. Inside she was flinched so tightly it was a wonder she hadn't shrunk, and it seemed to her haunted mind as if the air in the theatre had become dense and heavy.

'Of course I've got one,' she replied, hoping the flinch wasn't obvious in her voice and that the dense air would allow the passage of words. 'I've probably got a hundred, and yes, I'll find one, but Emily has been keeping a scrapbook for you, and she'll want to give you that herself.'

'Keeping a scrapbook for me?' Oliver echoed. 'What on earth do you mean?'

'Just that,' Clare told him, relaxing a little now and allowing herself a small smile at his bewilderment. 'It was her idea so we'll wait and let her explain, but I did tell you I've always answered any questions she's had about you, so it's not as if you'll be a complete stranger to her.'

'She'll be a complete stranger to me,' Oliver retorted, and now, feeling his pain, Clare released a little of hers.

'Let's not go there, Oliver,' she said, guilt over her abrupt reaction last night ensuring she spoke gently. 'What's done is done. Let's look ahead and work out what we can do to make the outcome best for both you and Emily.'

Oliver glared at her, but as other staff members were drifting into Theatre, the conversation had to cease.

He sorted through what he knew about the patient, a four-month-old baby girl with a complete atrioventricular septal defect, meaning the walls between the heart's right and left atria and right and left ventricles were incompletely formed so oxygenated blood from the lungs to the left atrium crossed to the right and went out again to the lungs, at far too great a pressure.

'Has she been suffering congestive heart

failure?' one of the nurses asked as Oliver studied the notes while waiting for the patient.

'Apparently not,' he said, 'which augurs well for us. That might be why Alex has decided to operate early rather than wait a couple of months for her to be stronger.'

The doors eased open and the gurney holding their patient was wheeled in, the infant looking so small, Clare felt a pang of concern, although she knew this operation was more or less routine for surgeons of the calibre of Alex and Oliver.

The team went smoothly into action, Clare more apprehensive than she'd been with baby Bob, probably because she was working with Alex for the first time.

'The tricky part is sorting out the valves—dividing the common valve we see in the defect into working mitral and tricuspid valves.'

Clare watched as Alex stood back to let Oliver do this delicate procedure—a sign that the team leader had the utmost confidence in his fellow. Alex must have known Oliver could be trusted to complete the intricate task successfully, and so it proved, his gloved hands handling the instruments swiftly and surely.

'Off pump.'

This time it was Oliver giving the order, the work on the little heart completed. Clare watched with the others, waiting nervously for the heart to beat, waiting, waiting. Alex massaged it, giving orders for drugs, then finally the heart moved of its own accord and a quiet cheer went up.

'We'll leave a pacemaker in her chest,' Alex said. 'The stitches we put in for the ventricular patch are very close to the tissue that supplies the electrical stimulus that makes the heart beat.'

The pacemaker fitted, Oliver closed the chest, and once again Clare couldn't help but notice the care he took to get the closure neat, and the gentle way he touched the infant's body.

He cares about his patients, she realised, although she'd known that back when they had lived together. He'd always spoken of them with genuine affection and part of the reason he had worked such long hours was because he went the extra mile for them—stayed at the hospital if there was any problem, or if the parents were overly concerned.

Would those qualities make him a good father?

Would professional care translate to personal care?

But was it caring she wanted for Emily from Oliver, or love?

Both, of course, but it was the love she wondered about. Could Oliver learn to love?

'I think she'll do well enough without ECMO, but be prepared for a call, Clare,' Alex was saying.

'I always am,' Clare told him. 'Now, what about baby Bob, am I taking him off the machine today?'

'You'll have to see what Angus thinks, but he was hopeful about it,' Alex told her. 'Oliver, maybe when you've changed, you and Clare could go and check it out.'

It was natural Alex would suggest they went, as both of them had been involved in Bob's operation, but the way Alex had paired their names made a shiver run down Clare's spine.

Oh, that it could be!

Dreamtime, Clare, get on with reality.

Oliver made his way into the locker room, wanting to change and be out of there before Clare came in. Bad enough that every time he saw her his body responded—something that had never happened to him before in professional situations, although he'd had relationships with colleagues—but to see her stripping off was asking too much of restraint.

Not that seeing him half naked appeared to affect her, for she'd come in, gone to her locker, picked up her mobile and appeared to be frowning at the message on it.

'Bad news?' he asked, a new anxiety banishing any thought of attraction. Bad news could involve Emily.

But Clare's rueful smile assured him it wasn't all that bad.

'In a way,' she said, coming across to him so she could speak quietly, yet pausing at arms length, tension coming in waves from her body for all she'd been smiling. 'I thought we had until Saturday to figure out a plan but here's a text from Em.' She handed him the phone. 'I assume you can understand nine-year-old texting.'

Oliver looked at the message which made no sense at all.

Nx wk not ths, cu 5 F

'"Next week not this, see you at five on Friday,"' Clare translated, making the original immediately obvious. 'Em had phoned earlier in the week about a party this Friday night but apparently she'd got the date wrong.'

'She's only nine and you're letting her go to parties?'

Oliver had to keep the demand to a whisper as other people were now in the room, but it was all he could do not to explode when Clare reacted with a smile.

How could she smile about a nine-year-old and parties?

'It's at the school,' she explained, 'in the

boarding house, in fact—a party to farewell the senior students. She'll be quite safe and I doubt it will go on later than nine—well, not for the junior school boarders anyway.'

'How was I supposed to know that?' he muttered but he was talking to himself, Clare having disappeared into one of the shower cubicles, returning only minutes later, fully clad in civvies once again.

'You ready?' she asked, and he was about to ask, Ready for what? when he remembered they were going to find Angus to check if baby Bob should come off ECMO.

Was he rattled by her presence, by the stuff that had happened between them last night, or was the knowledge that he had a daughter distracting him from his usual cool professionalism? It had to be the latter, Clare decided. Finding out something like that would distract the Sphinx. He was pulling a white coat over his striped business shirt and the sleeve caught.

Without thinking, she reached out to straighten it, but touching him was a mistake. Once again her body was responding to Oliver's, heating and swelling with a longing that she wondered if she could ever conquer.

Of course she could—she had only to remember how she'd reacted to his fingers on her breast and shame would be better than a cold shower.

Yet the longing remained, stirring up anger. The voice in the dream had been right—she *was* damaged goods.…

She headed out the door, away from any temptation to touch him again.

'So, we've got until Friday to come up with a plan?'

Oliver fell into step beside her as she headed for the PICU.

So much for attraction! He was obviously feeling nothing, and now she came to think of it, that kiss last night hadn't been about attraction on his part; it had simply been to prove a point—to prove marriage could work between them.

Unfortunately it had failed in the worst possible manner, but refusing to dwell on that again, she turned her full attention to Emily.

'I don't suppose we need a plan,' she admitted. 'I think I'll just tell her you're working here. It must be fate, I'll say. She'll like that bit. She'll think the gods were doing it just for her—for all I know she's been praying for this to happen, so maybe that's how it *did* come about.'

'And what about you? Do you believe it's fate?'

Clare turned to face him.

'I think it's just the most bizarre coincidence of all time, and I find the thought that there *might* be Fates who play around with the lives of humans to this extent scary.'

Extremely scary, she could have added, but she didn't want to sound paranoid, especially as Oliver was studying her with a strange expression on his face. Not exactly amused, but questioning somehow, and suddenly she was swamped, not with the attraction that had been confusing her so much—the bodily reactions— but with remembered love for this man.

At least, she hoped it was remembered love, not a new infection of the insidious disease, because love between them would be impossible.

'I don't know about the Fates playing with our lives,' he was saying, while Clare assured herself it had to be remembered love. She couldn't possibly *still* love him and there hadn't been time to fall in love with him again, especially as they'd been arguing for much of the time. 'But I could believe that this was meant to be. Why else would we have been brought together if not for Emily and me to get to know each other?'

'I can't answer that,' Clare said, aware she'd spoken shortly, but so thrown out of kilter by the feeling she'd had—the love idea—it was surprising she could speak at all. 'Let's forget all about it for the moment and see how Bob's doing.'

Oliver followed her into the PICU, but for once his mind wasn't totally on work. Something was upsetting Clare, something quite apart from introducing Emily to her father. Something from her past? He knew without a doubt that the attraction between them was as strong as ever, yet she'd ended the kiss in a panic, fear in her eyes....

Suspicion sneaked into his mind… She'd been married—not for long, a mistake…

Did he remember her saying that?

The hot rage that grew inside him was so unexpected and so strong he had to close his eyes lest they reveal his emotion.

You're only surmising, the few working neurones in his head reminded him. Now stop leaping to conclusions and think of your own problems. Think of Emily, of Clare in the context of a mother, not a lover.

'Are you concerned your relationship with Emily will change?' he asked, not realising where they were, by the monitors, and that Angus and a couple of nurses had probably heard the question.

'Who's Emily?' one of the nurses asked, and although Clare threw a scathing glance at Oliver, she ignored the question, asking one of Angus instead.

'Are we taking Bob off ECMO?'

'I think so,' Angus said. 'Originally I thought maybe he'd need another day but he's doing so well I think we should give him a go on his own. Let's take him into the procedure room and disconnect him, although I'll keep the cannulae in place just in case. You want to do it, Oliver?'

Oliver felt a swell of pride, enough to get his mind one hundred percent back on work. In some fellowship situations the fellow was a dogsbody, rarely given the opportunity to do much operating, but Alex had been definite that he worked differently—he actually wanted his fellows doing major surgery. And although disconnecting Bob from the ECMO machine wasn't major, it was still a responsibility that Angus, too, was giving to Oliver.

After the procedure was completed, Oliver spoke to the nurse who would monitor Bob, 'We'll need full blood values now, and continuous readings. Any sign that he's slipping back, just page me.'

He glanced at Angus, who nodded approval that Oliver had taken responsibility for the task right through to completion—sorting out the next stage of Bob's care.

Angus walked away, and a nurse wheeled

Bob back out into the PICU, but Oliver waited, watching Clare fiddle with her machine, securing lines and turning off the monitors.

'What do you do now?' he asked her. 'Hand it over to one of the techies to clean and sterilise?'

'Theoretically yes,' she said. 'I did that up in Theatre with the heart-lung machine, because they have the gear there to do it more efficiently than I could and they know the routine. But the ECMO machines, I like to do them myself. It's such a dicey thing, having a baby on one of them, that I want to know every one is working perfectly.'

He waited until she wheeled the machine out through a rear door, and would have liked to follow, just to see how it was made ready for the next patient.

Or was the real reason he wanted to follow because he wanted to spend longer with Clare, with the very professional Clare he felt he didn't know at all?

He'd told her he thought it was meant to be, them coming together so he could meet his daughter, but although the thought of that meeting generated equal amounts of excitement and sheer terror, his finding Clare again was a whole different ball game. Something deep inside him told him that this, too, was meant to be, but the emotional upheaval of the things he'd learned in Italy might have made him susceptible to such fancies.

And she obviously didn't share his sense of rightness about their meeting up again, mocking him when he suggested marriage, making it sound like an indecent proposal. Yet her response when they'd kissed was undeniable— the physical attraction that had flared between them from their first meeting had, if anything, become stronger.

Until…

He shook his head, admitting he had little knowledge of what went on inside Clare's head—any woman's head, for that matter—and here he was, about to get another female in his life.

Emily.

He checked on Bob before leaving the PICU,

went into the recovery room to find Alex with the baby girl they'd operated on earlier and, having assured himself he wasn't needed with either patient, wondered how he'd find Clare again. Suddenly the need to see a picture of his daughter had become urgent. He'd missed nine years and didn't want to miss another minute, but, of course, fate wasn't *that* co-operative, for Clare had disappeared.

CHAPTER FIVE

CLARE should have been relieved that Bob was off ECMO, and that the morning operation had gone well. She'd even managed a brief conversation about Emily with Oliver without falling to pieces, but none of these reassuring things lessened the agitation she was feeling. Inner agitation—twitchy; she felt twitchy.

Unwilling to go home lest she run into Oliver, she paced the tea room, pleased there was no-one to observe her agitation. Not much to attract the attention in a tea room, although there was a corkboard on one wall, covered in small notices, photos and postcards.

To divert herself from thoughts of twitches, attraction and Oliver in general—even from thoughts of Emily—she studied it.

The postcards must be from people who had worked with the team at some time, and she smiled to think where some of them had ended up—Italy, South Africa, even one from someone who'd moved on to her old hospital in Chicago. The photos were obviously of children who had been through the cardiac paediatric unit. All the photos were evidence of the success of cardiac surgery with the kids smiling and happy.

But it was a small notice decorated with balloons and streamers that caught Clare's interest.

Wanted—Bodies, it was headed, the words compelling attention.

Jimmie's Entertainment Unit is looking for people willing to give up some time be-tween now and Christmas Day to ensure that all the children in hospital over the fes-tive season are visited and treated to a little silliness.

Clare had to smile. These days professional clown 'doctors' were involved in most children's hospitals, but she knew from experience that volunteers were usually needed to augment the clowns' appearances, especially at Christmas when most entertainment units made a special effort.

Now here she was, back where she'd started. She'd taken out a pen to make a note of the contact number when she realised that the first meeting of the expanded entertainment group was tonight. A map at the bottom of the notice showed her how to get to the canteen in the other tower where the meeting would be held.

She had her pager, and another perfusionist was on duty, so there was no reason why she shouldn't join the troupe.

Although the performances would be close to Christmas when Emily would be home…so could she spare time away from her daughter? Or would Em be happy to join in?

Clare knew she would. Emily had often come to work with her, usually on weekends when Clare wasn't on duty but had wanted to call in to check on a particular patient, and Emily had enjoyed visiting the children's ward and chatting to the small patients. Best of all, she loved the babies and would stand outside the nurseries, peering through the glass, giving all the infants names as if they were her dolls.

Clare smiled at the thought, and for the first time since Oliver's stupid comment about marriage and the subsequent kiss had sent her spinning back into turmoil, she felt the dark cloud of unhappy memories lifting. In fact, the thought of performing again, even if it was only a bit part in a Christmas pantomime, was so therapeutic she made her way to the second tower with brisk, excited steps.

But no sooner had her spirits lifted than the cloud was back, and all because the first person she saw as she walked into the canteen was Oliver—large as life and twice as handsome—although she doubted it was his looks that made her heart race. Oliver could have looked like an ogre and he would still have the same effect.

'Did you come because you knew I'd be here? That's pretty close to stalking.'

She spat the words at him as soon as she drew near, so was disconcerted when he looked more puzzled than guilty.

'I'm sorry. I should have realised you'd be

interested but I didn't give it a thought. Becky, the unit secretary, was printing out the notice as I went past her desk and she more or less bullied me into coming. She made out it would be a good way for me, and other new members of the team, to meet some staff from other sections of the hospital, but what she was really doing, I think, was making sure someone from the unit would turn up.'

Idiot that I am, of course she'd be interested, Oliver was thinking to himself. And here he'd allowed Becky to talk him into it, because he hadn't been able to find Clare but had guessed she was still at the hospital, not at home.

'Okay, listen up, everyone.' Someone had stepped onto a table to open the meeting. 'I've put out a plca for extra people as I thought we might do a pantomime this year. We can have the Starlight Room for the main performance, but I wondered—if we have enough people—if we could run two or three similar shows, the second and third ones with smaller casts so they can perform in the wards for the children who can't be moved.'

Having worked with hospital entertainers from the time she was doing her drama course at university it was easy for Clare to imagine this proposal, the smaller units doing little more than appearing in costume in the wards. Oliver, however, looked confused.

'I'll explain later,' she whispered to him as the speaker introduced himself as Dr Droopy, then waved a hand to four other people who were the regular hospital clowns, introducing them in turn.

'I thought we'd do *Cinderella* which is a fairly easy pantomime, and so for the smaller performances we'd need only seven characters—Cinders herself, the prince, two ugly stepsisters and their mum, and a fairy godmother, plus an announcer-cum-voice-over-person. For the Starlight Room performance we need mice and jokers and extras for the ballroom scene—say, twenty if we can get them. So that's thirty-four in all—let's make it thirty-five minimum.'

He looked around.

'Now, there definitely aren't thirty-five people here, so I'd like you all to do some active recruiting, preferably within your own wards or units. That way, if you miss a rehearsal because you're on duty—and that's the only excuse I accept—there's someone handy to let you know what you missed.'

One of the other clowns was working his way through the gathering collecting names, contact numbers and places of work.

'Good,' he said when he reached Clare and Oliver. 'You two can be the nucleus of the cardiac department's show. Got anything against being an ugly stepsister?' he added to Oliver, who shrugged his shoulders as if it didn't matter, although he did wonder what he was getting himself into.

'You, of course,' the clown said to Clare, 'will be Cinders.'

'Cinderella is fair,' Clare pointed out. 'I can do ugly—I can be an ugly sister or even the stepmother.'

'No way,' the clown told her. 'We need *some* beauty in the show.'

He was flirting with her, Oliver realised, and against all logic his blood began to heat with something he hesitated to call jealousy but could be little else.

'Or fairy godmother—that's what you can be. We'll have a beautiful—' the fellow was saying now, but Clare cut him short.

'No way, the fairy godmother should be a bloke and a big bloke at that. I've done enough panto to know that. Anyway, you've got other names to gather and it seems to me that Dr Droopy is the boss and he'll decide who plays what.'

The clown gave her a disappointed look and moved on. Dr Droopy was asking everyone to try to recruit more bodies and announcing the next meeting the following week.

'Same time, same place,' he finished, and the crowd began to disperse.

'Actually, I don't think I'd be very good at pantomime,' Oliver said to Clare as they walked towards the door. 'I only came because Becky seemed to think someone from the unit should attend, but as you're here—'

Clare spun to face him.

'Don't you even *think* of backing out, Oliver

Rankin,' she said. 'In fact, given what Droopy said, you should be thinking of who you can con into joining us, not deserting a ship before it's even begun to sink!'

He had to smile at her vehemence.

'Hey, all I said was that I didn't think I'd be very good.'

Now she was smiling too.

'No one can be bad at pantomime,' she said. 'Making mistakes just makes it funnier—people will think you did it deliberately. Besides, everyone has to get involved in something over the festive season and anything is better than putting up balloons and tinsel.'

The enthusiasm in her voice died away at the end of the sentence, the change in her tone so obvious he had to ask.

'You don't like balloons and tinsel?'

She studied him, the smile gone now.

'Balloons I don't mind, even plastic evergreen I can handle—after all, I have to have a tree for Emily—but tinsel? It's like love, isn't it? Pretty and shiny when you first come across it, then before you know it, it's fallen down and people have walked over it and it's dirty and tawdry and done with.'

Oliver stared at her in dumb astonishment. Yes, ten years had passed since he'd last seen Clare, but bitterness had never been part of the eager, laughing, loving woman he had known. Without thinking, he reached out and touched his hand to her cheek, looking down into her dark eyes and seeing a stormy unhappiness he couldn't understand.

Although the memory of her face last night, white and fearful…

She blinked and moved away.

'Don't mind me,' she said, without looking back at him. 'Not a good time for me, Christmas, and with all the unrelenting jollity and goodwill it's hard to always put on an act.'

'Yet you're joining the panto,' he pointed out.

She spun back towards him.

'That's for the kids,' she said. 'Besides, being in the panto gives me a great excuse for not going to a lot of the parties that are usually on at the same time. With the panto you can plead rehearsals, costume fittings, costume sewing, a multitude of excuses that no-one ever questions.'

'Is it because we broke up when we did that you're so vehemently anti-Christmas?'

He *had* to ask.

She scanned his face, studying him for a moment, then shook her head.

'Maybe, though I'm not actually anti-Christmas—you can't be when you have a child—just anti-tinsel. You wait and see, two days after Christmas and the floors will be awash with it. It will be sticking to your shoe when you least expect it, and curled in corners of the elevators every time you go up and down. It's all-pervasive, everywhere—tired and dirty and worn.'

Like love?

Oliver wanted to pursue it, but sensed she was already regretting saying as much as she had. Was it their relationship that had made her feel this way, or her marriage? Although it wasn't relationships or marriage she was talking about; it was love.

And what did he know about love?

Not a single, solitary thing.

He shook his head as he followed her into the elevator and sneaked a glance into the corners for any rabid tinsel.

Clare believed in love. Love for her family, love for her friends, love for him at one time. Back when he'd known her, love had guided her life. So why had she taken this stand? How had love gone so bad for her?

A relationship that ended badly, a marriage that didn't work out—of course she'd be put off love. Yet could a woman as full of love as Clare had been set it aside like dirty tinsel?

He sighed inwardly, realising he didn't have a clue how this new Clare felt or thought.

But they'd be sharing a child. He *should* know her better.

'Will you have dinner with me?'

The question was out before he could give it proper consideration, and apparently it had surprised her almost as much as it had surprised him, for she was staring at him as if he'd suddenly spoken in tongues.

'Have dinner with you?'

Incredulity rattled the words.

Fortunately he had a perfect excuse.

'You could tell me more about Emily, and you have to remember it's been ten years since we saw each other. A lot has happened to both of us in ten years. Won't it make it easier for us, considering we're linked by Emily, if we fill in some of the blanks?'

'I guess.'

The response was so reluctant Oliver had to smile.

'Don't overwhelm me with enthusiasm now,' he said. 'We could go to the beach—down to Coogee. There are plenty of restaurants there to choose from, and if we sit on the pavement there'll be a sea breeze.'

They'd reached the ground floor so she didn't answer immediately, but once they were clear of the crowd exiting the elevator, she turned towards him.

'Do you know Sydney well, that you know about restaurants at Coogee?'

As questions went it was a fairly average one,

but it lit a minute spark of hope in Oliver's gut. At least she was going along with the idea.

'I stayed at a hotel in Coogee when I was here working with Alex earlier in the year. It was close and easier than looking for a furnished apartment.'

An ordinary conversation in the busy foyer of a children's hospital, yet Clare felt tension coil within her body. Oliver's excuse for dinner was to talk about Emily, but would he bring up the marriage idea again? Was he thinking he could discuss it over dinner in a public place where her reaction couldn't be too volatile?

Her heart quivered at the thought, although common sense decreed he was hardly likely to bring it up again after the way she'd pushed him off last night.

'Don't look so stressed—it's only dinner,' he was saying. 'We both have to eat.'

She nodded, agreeing they both had to eat, assuring herself she could get through a dinner with him without falling apart.

'This is really stupid,' she told him, pretending to a lightness she was far from feeling. 'Here we are, once in a relationship together, and behaving with the formality of two people discussing a blind date.'

'Well, it feels a bit that way to me,' Oliver said, so quietly Clare wondered if she'd really heard him.

Blind dates were awkward things, and Oliver, overloaded with a magnetic attraction for women, could never have felt that awkwardness.

Could he?

'Do you have to check on Bob?' he asked, and when she nodded he continued, 'Then I'll go home to get the car and meet you back here—when? Half an hour?'

'Half an hour's good,' she said, although, contrarily, given that this was far from a date, she had an urge to make the time longer so she could rush home and change out of the neat and practical jeans and polo shirt she'd worn to work this morning.

Ridiculous reaction! Here she was, going out with the man to talk about their daughter, and she was worrying about how she looked?

It was because of the way her heart had reacted

when he'd mentioned dinner. With that one casual invitation she'd regressed to the twenty-year-old she'd been when she first met Oliver, when he'd come into her life and swept her off her feet. Her heart had raced, her blood heated, and hope had lightened her entire body.

She made her way to the PICU, wishing she hadn't thought about teenage-type reactions because now her heart was aching with the remembered love she'd had for Oliver—love that she'd thought would last for ever....

There was a restaurant set on a cliff top just along the ocean-side walk north of Coogee, Oliver remembered. It would be quieter there than a sidewalk café. He tried to remember the name of it, but drew a blank. However, it was unlikely it would be busy on a Wednesday night so they could take a chance on getting in.

And why did he want to take Clare somewhere quieter than a sidewalk café?

The question was an obvious one, but no easy answer came to mind.

'We're going where?' she asked when, once

she was settled in the car, he tried to explain about this particular place.

'Just along the cliffs from Coogee,' he told her, 'but the problem is, I walked there when I went before and, while I assume you can drive, I don't know the name of the place, so I can't look up the address. Do you mind a walk?'

'What *kind* of a walk?' she demanded, and he turned to smile at her.

'Maybe a mile at the most—you know me, hardly the walking type. In fact, I remember you nearly killing me walking up and down the hills at your farm. My feet were made for pushing accelerators and brake pedals, not for tramping around sodden paddocks with grass a foot high.'

She laughed and it seemed to Oliver as if his chest had filled with helium, so light did he feel.

Clare's laughter, one of the first things he'd learned to—

To *love* about her?

Had he loved her? Loved her and not wanted

to admit it because he was determined not to be undermined by some indefinable emotion?

Is that why losing her had been so painful?

'What's wrong? Are we lost?'

He slid the car into a parking spot close to where the ocean-front walk began, and turned to look at her.

'Nothing's wrong,' he said, but he wasn't so sure because his mind was still stuttering around over the possibility that maybe what he'd felt for Clare all those years ago *had* been love, and that he'd just not known it because love wasn't something that had featured in his life up to that point.

'Come on, we walk from here,' he told her, hurrying to open her car door, but she was already out, still frowning slightly at him, as if she'd read something in his face earlier and wasn't at all convinced by his answer to her questions.

Why had laughing at the memory of a happy time they'd had together made him frown?

Clare joined him on the path that led up a

grassy slope towards the cliff top at the northern end of the lovely curved beach.

And was he still annoyed at whatever made him frown that he was striding out now as if they needed to reach the top in record time?

Not that she couldn't match his strides. She'd kept her fitness up in Chicago, loving the walks she and Emily would take around the lake. The freedom of movement and fresh air had relaxed and invigorated her after long, and often tense, sessions in Theatre, but as well as that, the walks had been a special bonding time with her daughter.

But in the present, in the fraught and nervous now, as Clare fell into step beside Oliver, she regretted agreeing to this outing. *She* might know it wasn't a date but her body wasn't convinced, reacting when their arms brushed, heating when he touched her shoulder and pointed out to sea.

'Are those dolphins out there?'

She stopped and stood beside him, her eyes following the direction of his finger, and after a few seconds three sleek forms broke the surface of the water, way out beyond the breakers—three dolphins frolicking in the sea.

'They're beautiful, aren't they?' she breathed, speaking quietly because she'd always loved these lissom creatures, feeling some kind of kinship with them, although why she didn't know.

'You told me once you thought you'd been a dolphin in a previous life,' Oliver said. He'd spoken just as quietly as she had, yet a strange excitement ripped through her body.

No, no, no, no, no! You can't go all gooey just because he remembered a chance remark. We were together five years—more if you took in the courting time before she moved in with him. He *had* to remember some bits of it.

But the excitement refused to be dampened, so as they moved on Clare made sure she walked just slightly behind him, so they couldn't brush arms, or accidentally touch in any way.

The view from the top of the path was brilliant, the sea at dusk an inky blue, contrasting with the white of the plumes of water that flew into the air where the waves battered endlessly against the cliff.

'I do love the smell of the sea,' Clare murmured, stopping to take the salty air deep into her lungs, but as Oliver stopped beside her, her nerves grew taut and a deep yearning to be held—and hold—hollowed out her body.

Or maybe it was hunger.

It had better be hunger. Holding and being held had ended in disaster, she reminded herself.

She moved, heading along the path, berating herself for her stupidity in agreeing to have dinner with Oliver, because being with him was just too confusing.

They followed the path to where the sea had gained purchase in the land, hollowing out a deep inlet, and perched above it the restaurant, blending in with the rocky landscape, only visible because it was well lit.

'Inside, or on the verandah?' the waiter asked when they entered the building.

'Verandah!'

They answered together and Clare had to smile at their reaction, remembering they'd always preferred outdoor dining when there was an option. The waiter led them to a table on a deck cantilevered out over the water below, water that surged and retreated, moving restlessly but without the fury of the waves that broke against the cliffs.

Restless? Was that how she felt? Did that explain the hollow feeling?

Of course it didn't...

Then what did?

'A glass of wine or something soft?'

Oliver looked at her over the wine list he was studying, but his eyes seemed to be asking a different question, a thousand questions—how was she, where had she been, what had been happening in her life...?

As if eyes could convey that much.

'Lime and soda, thanks,' she said, adding, 'I'm starving,' as she opened the menu and started to read the choices.

'Balmain bugs with chilli sauce.'

The waiter had returned for their drinks order but Clare felt he might as well take the food one at the same time; that way they'd be served more quickly. They could eat and leave and she could sort out all the confusion inside her once she got home.

She was wondering where the conversation should go when Oliver spoke.

'I've spent the past few years in the UK, then I went to Italy before I came back to Australia.' Oliver wasn't sure why he'd come out with this in the pause following the waiter's departure with their orders. There'd certainly been no conversational lead into it, but suddenly the words were out there.

Because they'd come to talk about their daughter?

Because subconsciously it was disturbing him that Emily shared his unhappy heritage?

Clare appeared startled by the conversation, then she frowned.

'Holiday or more than that?'

'I went to the village where my mother grew up. Ever since Owen told me I wasn't his son— and you'd remember *that* fun time in my life— I've been torn between wanting to know more about my father and denying him completely.'

'Denial was winning when I knew you,' Clare reminded him, but gently because she remembered how shattered Oliver had been at the time.

Oliver shrugged.

'I probably should have stuck to it,' he said, sorry now that he'd brought it up. Surely he could have made conversation about their patients, or the weather, or the ocean—anything!

'Bad stuff?'

The dark eyes still studied him, assessing—familiar.

'Not that bad. Pretty average really, although not as bad as Owen had made out when he told me. His version was that my father could have been any one of a dozen young local men. He claimed it was because of my mother's reputation in the village that her family sent her to the relatives in Australia.'

He paused; then, with his eyes fixed firmly on Clare's lovely face, he added, 'Do you wonder I didn't want children? Didn't want to pass on that kind of legacy?'

She shook her head, her eyes almost black in the shadowy light, dark with sympathy.

'So, did you find your father?'

He heard her empathy in the words and re-membered how supportive she'd been when he'd found out about Owen. She'd wrapped him in her love and then, within months, he'd rejected her.

Damn it all, the conversation was bringing back too many memories.

Still, he could hardly stop now—hardly not answer her question.

'I found out who he was—meeting him was something else altogether. Neither he, nor anyone in the village, not even my grandpar-ents who are still alive, wanted anything to do with me.'

'I'm sorry it was a bad experience,' Clare said, pain for him so acute she was having trouble breathing. Oliver had suffered one rejection when he'd learned Owen wasn't his father; for this to happen...

'You hear so many good stories about people finding their birth parents that you forget it doesn't work out for everyone,' she added. 'Can you put it behind you now? Go forward rather than looking back?'

He didn't reply, studying her instead, surely not trying to read anything behind the words.

'I mean it, Oliver,' she added. 'That wasn't a trite remark but genuine sympathy because I know how much that part of your past worried you.'

Still no response, so she ploughed on. 'But the past *is* past. Now, let's not spoil a good meal by dwelling on it. Look forward, go forward.'

He smiled at her, and for the first time in her life she understood the phrase *the world stood still*, for it happened to her right then and there. It was a smile, no more, but although she tried her best not to respond to it, her body ignored her, sending waves of heat simmering along her nerves, twitching at her muscles and tightening her lungs.

No!

It won't work.

You learned that last night.

Get over it.

'You're right,' he said, 'and I'm sorry for burdening you with that business, but you were there when I first found out that I wasn't Owen's son, so it seemed natural to tell you.'

Natural?

Forget heat and twitching muscles, woman, and get with the situation here.

Fortunately the waiter arrived, giving her an excuse to stop considering anything but food. She turned her attention to the plate in front of her.

'It looks and smells delicious.'

She glanced up at Oliver as she spoke and, because he was so familiar, even ten years on, she began to relax.

'Thank you,' she said, 'for suggesting this, for bringing me here. It's a magical place. I lived near the lake in Chicago and Em and I walked there often, but it's not like being near the sea.'

Oliver watched as she used the silver tweezers to pull the flesh out of the bug's case. She was concentrating on the task, the corner of her bottom lip caught between her teeth. 'Look forward, go forward,' she'd said, but could anyone completely wipe away the past?

Could she, whatever it was?

Successfully removing the meat, she cut a chunk off and popped it in her mouth, sighing blissfully when she chewed and swallowed.

'Aren't you going to eat?' she demanded when she caught him watching her. She waved her cutlery towards his plate where a thick slice of rare Wagyu beef shared a plate with chargrilled vegetables. 'It looks good.'

'I'll eat,' he assured her, cutting into the beef. 'But tell me about you. Where is "forward" for Clare Jackson? Where are you looking to go?'

Dark eyes flicked towards him, unreadable, then she concentrated on sorting another mouthful of food.

'Strange question, when I've just begun a new job, but since you ask, I aim to be the top paediatric perfusionist in Australia. That's where I'm going. I'm going to be on the board of the Australasian Society of Cardio-Vascular Perfusionists, and I'm going to train and examine and be involved with the development of the career path for future perfusionists.'

He had to laugh, shaking his head at the same time, because she sounded so totally convinced that this would all happen.

'Sounds like a plan,' he teased and watched a faint colour rise in her cheeks.

'It's been my plan for some time now,' she said quietly, and he wondered just what had happened in her life that she'd needed to define herself again—to find a new career path, however unusual, and to aim for the top in it.

The marriage that was a mistake?

Whatever had generated her reaction last night?

He cut some more steak and chewed on it, wondering at the same time, thinking...

The past is past, she'd said, and while Oliver was willing to let their shared past lie where it was, he couldn't help but wonder about the past he hadn't shared with her.

'And you?'

Because he was still thinking of Clare's past, the words made little sense until she added,

'Where are you going? You've this fellowship with Alex—that's, what, a year? And after that?'

After that?

He hadn't thought that far.

Well, he had. Originally he'd hoped to work with Alex, then, as the dutiful only child of a mother who was getting older, move back to Melbourne, taking up a senior position in one of the paediatric cardiac surgical units there—

'Hey, you're supposed to be telling me, not just thinking about it,' Clare reminded him. 'This is regular dinner conversation—you ask a question, I reply, then I ask one and you reply, remember?'

'Who knows?' he replied, dodging the issue, because his feelings towards his mother, a woman who had lied so often to him, were far too complex to go into over dinner. Too complex for him to think about most of the time, which is why he considered duty rather than love when he thought about her. 'Things happen, plans change. We've the perfect example of that with

Emily. Obviously now I've got to factor her in, factor you in.'

Had his voice sounded strained that Clare reached out her hand and caught at his fingers, squeezing them lightly?

'We'll work it out,' she said quietly.

And suddenly he realised just how good it was to sit with Clare like this, doing nothing more exciting than eating dinner in a special place. He even found himself relaxing.

'Your family?' he asked. 'They're well?'

'They're all in Queensland now,' Clare told him, but he sensed the question had been ill-timed, for suddenly her voice sounded strained and tight. But as he watched he saw her rally, her spine straightening and colour returning to her cheeks. 'My dad died and we sold the farm. My brothers bought a property on the Darling Downs in Queensland—they do some cropping and raise Black Angus. They're lovely beasts, the Black Angus, docile and really good doers, and best of all, as far as my brothers are concerned, there's no twice-daily milking.'

'I'm sorry to hear about your father. I know how close you were.'

It was his turn to offer comfort, turning her hand in his to gently press her fingers.

She took back her hand and shrugged.

'These things happen,' she said, but her voice told him she wasn't over her father's death, that it still hurt her more than she would admit. He looked around, seeking distraction, wanting to regain the mood of pleasant companionship he'd felt earlier.

'During the day you can sometimes see big kingfish in this inlet,' he said, apropos of nothing.

'You'll have to show me some time. We could bring Em,' she replied, and though that, too, was probably nothing more than a throwaway line, the thought of coming here again with Clare sent a surge of excitement through him.

Though the 'bringing Emily' part brought back all the fears and insecurities that had been nagging at him since he'd learnt he had a daughter.

He called for the bill, paid it and they left,

Emily not discussed at all, and an uncomfortable silence stretching between them.

Was Clare, too, feeling discomfort in the silence that she chatted on about their patients and the operations, sticking solely to work talk the whole way home? Then, as he drove into the garage and stopped the car, she was out in a flash, thanking him and taking off through the shadowed garden as if chased by demons.

By the time he reached their shared landing, she was gone, her door shut and the muted sound of a radio or television coming from behind it.

CHAPTER SIX

No OPERATIONS, just patients to see—regular
check-ups, query patients referred from GPs,
patients in for various tests. Oliver found the
change refreshing, enjoying again the interac-
tion between the children and their parents.

His final patient of the day was, by chance—
there it was again—a nine-year-old girl, a little
charmer who'd been born with a partial AVSD
which had been repaired when she was twelve
months old.

'I really don't need to be still seeing a specialist,' she told him with the utmost confidence,
'but it makes Mum feel better so I do it.'

She talked on, seeming to know a great deal
about her operation, explaining, when he mentioned this, 'Oh, I'm in a chat room with some
other kids who've had heart surgery. We talk
about all kinds of things, compare scars and

stories of how nearly we were to dying, although I think most of us exaggerate that part.'

Did all nine-year-olds use the word *exaggerate* with such confidence? Oliver wondered, upgrading his image of his daughter from a just-past-starting-school stage to an almost teen.

I'll never cope. The panic-stricken thought rendered him momentarily speechless, but fortunately his new young friend was now telling him about a boy on the chat list that she thought fancied her, though meeting him might be difficult as he lived in England.

'Dr Rankin worked in England—he might know him.' Was the nine-year-old's mother trying to stem the flow of conversation?

And how likely was that in a country of more than forty million people? He was about to point out the impossibility when another panic struck him. This nine-year-old girl—a child—had a boy who fancied her.

Not *his* daughter! he decided savagely, but now the child was telling him the name of her boy friend—two separate words, Oliver told himself, not one—and the name was ringing a bell.

'Is he from Leeds?' he asked, getting back into the conversation with some difficulty.

'Yes, he is,' the delighted child replied. 'Do you know him?'

Oliver shook his head. This was taking coincidence too far. He refused to believe in Fates that pushed human lives around on some kind of cosmic chessboard, but—

'I actually operated on him a few years ago,' he admitted. 'Like you, he had an AVSD when he was an infant, but he had a full separation, not a partial like yours, and he needed another op a year or so ago to stop his mitral valve leaking.'

'What's he like?' the excited girl demanded. 'Is he as good-looking as his picture? Does he really have a tattoo?'

Oliver closed his eyes. Nine-year-old girls could not *possibly* be turned on by boys with tattoos. He refused to believe it.

'I don't remember a tattoo,' he managed to reply, then he turned the conversation off the boy in Leeds by reminding his patient he had to examine her, and keeping the talk to purely professional matters.

'I'll tell him you're my new doctor. He'll be so excited,' the girl told him as she left, while her mother, waiting until her daughter was out of earshot, smiled at Oliver in a harried kind of way.

'She's got two older brothers and, believe me, driving them around to sporting practice and games is a small price to pay for having boys. The elder one is thirteen now, and I swear he's not even aware girls exist, except for the ones who play soccer with him.'

Oliver went back into the office, sank down into his chair and rested his head on the desk. He thought of banging it against it, but he'd done that one other afternoon and knew it didn't help.

How could he possibly be a father to a nine-year-old girl? He didn't know the first thing about fatherhood and, never having had a sister, knew even less about young girls. Images he had of pretty little things playing quietly in a corner with their dolls or perhaps doing scales on a piano were obviously so out-of-date he needed a crash course of some kind.

He'd start with Clare. Forget marriage, forget attraction; they had to concentrate on Emily. Having kept his daughter from him all this time, Clare owed him, and she could begin repayment by bringing him up-to-date on what his daughter loved and hated, thought about, dreamed of and generally believed in as far as nine-year-old life was concerned.

He found Clare sitting on Becky's desk, chatting away about something—clothes probably. Hell, did the clothes thing begin in childhood with women? Would he have to learn about child fashion as well? He'd have to make a list.

No, Clare would have to make a list. Emily's likes and dislikes—that kind of thing.

'Are you heading home?' he asked her, then added in a very firm voice before she had a chance to refuse, 'We could walk together.'

'Very masterful,' Clare murmured to Becky, and the two women smiled, further raising the aggravation he was feeling towards the whole female sex. But Clare had slid off the desk and showed every sign of being willing to walk with him, for which he should be pleased.

Not so. Walking with her, even in a reasonably crowded hospital corridor, reminded him of the other aggravating aspect of the female species—the fact that they could give out some kind of emanations that made the coolest of men feel warmth building in their bodies, and carnal thoughts slipping into their minds.

He forced himself to think of the purpose of this walk.

'Docs Emily think boys with tattoos are cool?' he asked, or maybe demanded, for Clare stopped walking and turned to him with so much astonishment on her face he felt totally stupid.

'I can explain,' he said as the elevator doors opened and they stepped into the crowd inside.

'I'm sure you can,' Clare told him quietly, 'but perhaps not here.'

So they rode down in silence, which wasn't good for the emanation thing, but at least battling it took his mind off Emily for a few minutes.

Should she apologise for her behaviour last night? But how could she apologise without some explanation? And how could she explain that telling Oliver of her father's death had brought back so many bad memories she'd barely been able to breathe?

Clare stood beside him, trying to convince herself that guilt over her abrupt departure last night was making her feel so fidgety. It couldn't possibly be desire—not when she knew anything between them would be impossible.

And Oliver only wanted to walk with her to talk about Emily.

She took the lead in case the conversation didn't go that way.

'What's this about boys with tattoos?' she asked as they left the hospital and headed through the grounds towards the traffic lights at the corner of their street.

'I've been talking to a nine-year-old girl,' he replied, his voice so laden with doom she had to hide a smile as she turned towards him, relaxed now that the conversation *was* about Em.

'Ah! A nine-year-old girl who fancies a boy with tattoos?'

The lights changed and they crossed, jostled to and fro by the mass of people, so it wasn't until they were alone on their street that Oliver answered her.

'She thinks *he* fancies her! Please tell me our daughter isn't into boys! I realise fancying boys or them fancying her will come into the picture sometime and I don't know how the hell a father handles things like that, but I thought I'd have a kind of breaking-in period.'

'I think you're safe with Em,' Clare told him, her heart filled with joy at this evidence that Oliver was actually considering himself a father, before he'd even met his daughter. 'At the moment she's horse obsessed and I've encouraged that because to me it's better than being clothes obsessed, and believe me, some nine-year-olds are. They know the cool brands, all of which are expensive, and won't be seen dead in anything else.'

'I think I need a list,' he announced.

He thinks he needs a list? Clare muddled over it for a while, then had to ask.

'What kind of list?'

'An Emily list—what she likes and doesn't like. Food and games and stuff, then perhaps another list of things she does, and hopes and dreams...'

'And pop stars and TV stars and boy bands and clothes,' Clare added, smiling now at the thought of the endless lists she could make out. 'It won't work,' she added, although the warm feeling inside her grew stronger, because Oliver cared enough to ask for lists. 'Nine-year-old girls don't have strong allegiances. What or who she likes this week could be completely different next week. It makes buying presents very tricky because you might think she's still reading school stories and she's decided they're old hat—that is *not* a nine-year-old's expression but one of mine—and she's wanting some other book altogether.'

'I'll never be able to do it,' Oliver said, so much despair in his voice Clare had to touch him. She reached out to pat his arm, feeling the muscle beneath his shirt, feeling all the things she still felt when she touched Oliver, no matter how unbelievable that might be.

'Of course you will—you're good with children.'

'Other people's children,' he reminded her as they turned in through their gate. 'What if I cook dinner and you write lists. Or if you don't like the thought of lists you could just sit there and talk about what she thinks and does and talks about so I can get a sense of her.'

He was following her up the stairs as he made the dinner suggestion, and whether it was the idea of sitting in Oliver's kitchen while he cooked dinner, or his presence behind her on the stairs, she didn't know, but a shiver of apprehension had slithered up her spine and left the nerves in her back tingling.

To be honest, other nerves were tingling as well—deep-seated nerves—so relief flooded through her when he added, 'Oh, no, I can't do that. I haven't shopped, and although Alex's wife left the basics in the flat for me, they certainly don't run to cooking dinner.'

Clare had reached the landing at the top of the steps and was unlocking her door when he joined her.

'Is there somewhere close by that we can eat?' he asked. 'Actually, that's a better idea. You can talk and I can make the lists—or take notes—about whatever I might need to think about later.'

He took her arm and turned her back towards the stairs.

'Come on.'

'Right now? Forget it. I am going inside. I'm going to kick off my shoes and have a long cold drink and then a long cool shower. Besides, you bought dinner for me last night.'

'Well, tonight we can go Dutch—and you're right, if we shower and change we'll be fresher. I noticed in the notes Annie—that's her name, isn't it?—left for me that there are a couple of restaurants within walking distance, casual places with good food, she said. I'll pick the closest, is that all right?'

Oliver knew he was pushing Clare, but for all that he believed she'd tried to contact him about Emily, he still felt he was the injured party here. After all, *she'd* left *him*, and he deserved a little consideration.

'You have to eat,' he reminded her, 'and you can't deny me the opportunity to learn as much as I can about Emily before I meet her, now can you?'

She studied him for a moment, her hand still on the key in the door.

'As long as that's all it's about, Oliver,' she said sternly. 'No more kisses. Emily's future is far too important to me to risk disturbing it with muddled thinking.'

Oliver was about to smile but caught it just in time. Best not to look triumphant, but he couldn't help but comment on her words.

'You're saying our kisses muddle your thinking?'

'Of course they muddle my thinking,' she said crossly. 'They always have, and now you're back, it's even more disturbing. I mean, we hardly know each other, and there's other stuff—a *lot* of other stuff. It's impossible...'

With that she flung open her door and stepped inside, her back to him so he could afford to smile, for if her words weren't confirmation of the fact that she was still as much attracted to him as he was to her, what were they?

'How long do you need to get ready?' he called after her. 'Shall I knock in half an hour?'

'Okay' came the reply as the door closed between them, and although it had all the enthusiasm of someone agreeing to an enema, Oliver felt a lurch of excitement.

He'd rushed Clare with the marriage suggestion, but it was the perfect solution. She'd obviously suffered some trauma in their years apart—either in her marriage or maybe in childbirth—but together they could sort it out, especially as the attraction between them was as strong as ever.

They'd put the past with all its hurts behind them, and begin again. Married! That way, he could be part of his daughter's life, taking up his rightful place as her father, and Clare could continue to handle the main parenting stuff, just as she'd been doing for nine years.

He ignored a slight qualm of conscience about this imagined arrangement, assuring himself that in time he'd grow into the parenting role and all would be well. In the meantime, he was going out to dinner with Clare, and if he remembered the map Annie had drawn, their route would take them through the park, and if walking through a park in the moonlight didn't soften Clare's attitude to kissing, he didn't know what would.

He's doing it again, Clare admitted to herself as she kicked off her shoes, then dropped into an armchair, leaning back against the headrest and letting the tensions of the day ease from her body. Rushing me headlong into something without giving me time to think. That's how we got together in the first place—attraction, bed, let's move in together.

Yes, he needed and deserved to learn more of Emily, but she knew him well enough to realise he hadn't given up on the marriage idea.

Obviously there would have to be a relationship of some kind between them—they shared a daughter—but knowing Oliver he'd use that as an excuse to push or pull her somewhere she didn't want to go.

Couldn't go.

The thought caused an ache in her heart. She'd reached out and touched him earlier and, touching him, had known she loved him. It had been as simple as that. No need to question whether it had never gone away, her love for Oliver, or whether this was new love. It didn't matter because it was simply there, deep in her heart, and there it would stay no matter what.

She almost sighed, then realised she seemed to be spending a lot of time sighing these days, so shut it off and straightened in the chair. Loving Oliver might be a fact, but it was an irrelevant one—a secret she had to keep to herself.

It was also a secret she couldn't allow to have any bearing on the decisions she would make about Emily's future.

Right now she had to think clearly of the future, not the past, and of practical matters, not love. For Emily's sake she had to set aside her personal issues and concentrate on the best outcome for her daughter.

She nodded acknowledgement of this decision and rose out of the chair. Time to shower and dress for dinner, to arm herself against whatever seductive wiles Oliver might choose to use. Though to be fair, it probably wasn't his fault that his body held such a powerful attraction to hers.

Nor were her memories his fault.

Perhaps if she remembered those two things, she could have a normal, adult conversation with him.

'You look great!'

Three words, a conventional, probably meaningless compliment, and her resolution about the seductive wiles of his body dissolved like sugar in hot water. And so much for deciding not to put on any make-up. Given the limited time and the decision to ignore attraction, all she'd done was shower, pull on a long cool summer dress, then whip her hair up into a clasp on the top of her head, again for coolness.

'You clean up okay yourself.'

She returned the compliment, but made sure he *knew* it was nothing more than polite conversation by turning from him to lock her door.

In fact, he'd cleaned up so far ahead of okay that for a moment he'd stolen her breath—and her resolve. He was wearing a dark blue shirt that for some perverse reason made his eyes seem greener, and stone-washed jeans that hugged his hips like a lover, revealing the swell of his butt and thick muscled thighs.

'So…Emily, horses, you say. Does she have a horse?'

They were across the road and on the path leading through the park, the lights already on, although it was barely dusk.

Great, Emily conversation. Clare knew she could handle this, although she now realised that any time she was with Oliver, especially alone with Oliver, was like walking across a floor littered with broken glass—shards of broken dreams?—so she was always aware of having to tread especially carefully.

What was the question?

Horses.

'Does she have a horse? Are you kidding? Do you have any idea how much the care and feeding of a horse costs? Different in the country, where a horse can live out in a paddock and eat grass, but in a city? They have to be stabled and exercised and brushed and combed and fed, daily tasks beyond the ability of a nine-year-old who also has to go to school.'

Oliver listened to the words, but part of his brain was considering his companion—how beautiful she looked in the long, swishing dress with its fitted top cupping her full breasts, and the thin shoulder straps revealing the smooth golden skin of her shoulders and the pure, taut lines of her neck.

Emily. They were talking about Emily.

'How much?' he asked, and Clare stopped in mid-stride to turn and face him.

'How much what?' she asked, her dark eyes

shadowed to almost black, and genuinely puzzled.

'How much does it cost to keep a horse in the city?'

She frowned at him, then shook her head.

'I've no idea—not in actual, up-to-date figures—but I know it's a lot. But the reality isn't the cost of keeping the horse, but a nine-year-old's forever changing goals and passions. Next year—forget that, next week—it might be swimming or hang gliding or who knows what. For the moment, the school provides an adequate outlet for the horse mania. Students who are interested ride one afternoon a week, and there's the horse camp in the holidays. If she keeps riding, and does well at it, proving she's committed to it, then later on I'll think about a horse.'

'*We'll* think about a horse,' Oliver corrected, but the conversation had puzzled him enough for him to ask, 'How do you know these things about changing goals and passions and nine-year-olds? Are there books?'

Clare smiled, such an open, delighted smile

it made something stir inside Oliver's chest. He hoped he wasn't back to ectopic heartbeats.

'There are books—hundreds of books—but I was a girl myself, and though at nine a horse would have been an acceptable passion for someone who lived on a farm, I wanted to be a surfer like my brothers. I nagged and nagged for a surfboard for my birthday but Mum and Dad had enough sense to start me off on an old one of Steve's. I was still learning to stand on it when a friend got a pair of hamsters and surfing was forgotten in the bid to become a hamster tycoon. I've forgotten what came next, but Mum no doubt remembers every one of my enthusiasms—all the things I'd absolutely die if I didn't get, have, try.'

Had his face betrayed his reaction that she reached out and grasped his arm?

'Oh, Oliver, I'm sorry. I forgot what a miserable excuse for a childhood you had.'

He stepped towards her and slipped his free arm around her shoulders.

'Don't be sorry about your happiness—it's beautiful to see,' he told her, then he kissed her, very lightly, on the temple, where a blue vein pulsed beneath her golden skin. 'And that's a caress, not a kiss,' he added as he turned away, steering both of them along the path, but keeping his arm firmly around her shoulders.

It was obvious the physical attraction between them was as strong as ever, however much she might shy away from their kisses and make rules about not kissing again. So surely if he promoted the attraction, even with a casual hand holding their bodies close, it would be a good thing....

A good thing when she'd flinched and paled and drawn away from him in fear or pain?

He shook his head, determined this night would be different. This night would be about Emily.

It was wrong, walking with Oliver like this. It made Clare think all kinds of things she shouldn't think, like might not being married to him, being a family with him and Em, be a good idea.

She forced herself to think of how she'd shrunk away from him when he'd kissed her,

her movement sheer instinctive fear. And how she'd fled from him last night, afraid it might happen again.

No, marrying Oliver—marrying anyone—was an impossible dream.

'There's the restaurant.' He pointed ahead, and Clare felt a sense of relief that the far-too-intimate walk was nearly at an end. Although they still had to walk back.

'I'll pay tonight,' she said. 'You got the bill last night and—don't argue—I'm a working woman and pay my own way.'

'When I've not contributed one penny to my daughter's upkeep for nine years? Forget it!'

She glanced at him, about to argue that he'd said they'd go Dutch when she saw the set expression on his face. The argument died on her lips as she imagined how emotionally overwhelming it must be to suddenly discover you have a nine-year-old child.

If they were married, she could be more supportive to him, help him in his dealings with Em.

And happily go to bed with him?

She was back on the field of broken glass again.

'Have you been here before?'

The nice, normal question pulled her out of useless speculation.

'No, but I believe it's very popular with hospital staff. Oh, damn, I hadn't thought about that, and here's me hoping to keep any relationship between us quiet until after we've got Em sorted out.'

Oliver stopped walking on the pavement outside Scoozi, and looked at her.

'You used not to worry about every little thing. In fact, you plunged into life as if welcoming the rocks as much as you welcomed the diamonds. Is it motherhood or something else that makes you so cautious now?'

Something else, maybe both—but neither was a reply she intended giving.

'Have you considered it might just be age?' she said as lightly as she could, given the memories he'd stirred up again.

He studied her for a moment longer, then shook his head.

'Age doesn't change a personality,' he said quietly, then he took her elbow and guided her into the restaurant, agreeing with the waiter who met them that, yes, the garden courtyard would be a lovely place to eat this evening.

Clare looked around her, accepting that some of the other patrons would inevitably be hospital staff but pleased that no-one from their team was dining there tonight. So Emily would be a safe topic of conversation; actually, Emily would be the only safe topic, given the physical tension that still stretched between herself and Oliver. Some of her colleagues were already aware she had a daughter; in fact, Alex had already met Emily, but now that Oliver had come into the picture, explaining *that* relationship—well, that was too complex to consider right now.

'Tell me about the school,' Oliver suggested, as if he, too, had decided his daughter was to be the focus of their conversation.

'It's a great place—unbelievable. I'd heard about it over the years because Mum's youngest brother lives on a property out in western New South Wales and his daughter Caitlin has been a border there since she was about the same age Emily is now. Over the years, we've stayed with Uncle Ken in holidays so Em already knew Caitlin, and it was Em who decided, when we came back to Australia, that that's where she'd like to go.'

'Is it some distance from where we live? Is that why you opted for the boarding option?'

Clare shook her head, then paused as the waiter set down their drinks and took their food order.

'It's a ten-minute ride in a taxi, or if she was a day girl a school bus would collect her outside the door,' she explained. 'But as I think I told you, Mum lived with us up until now so she was always there for Em. However, it was time we let Mum go back to her own life, and although I work fairly regular hours there are times I'm called out at night or work late and I couldn't have Em being on her own. Weekly boarding gives us the best of two worlds as she has friends among the other boarders to do things with after school hours, and we have the weekends together.'

Together.

Although he'd felt he'd been handling this emotional bombshell quite well up to now, that one word caused such pain he actually winced.

Go forward, he repeated to himself. Think of the future, not the past.

'The text message—did it say what time you could collect her?' he asked. 'I was so impressed by your ability to translate it, I've forgotten what it said.'

'Soon after five,' Clare replied, then her dark eyes met his and she studied him for a moment before adding, 'I'd suggest you come with me, but that's too sudden. Give me time to get her home and tell her, then can we leave it up to her?'

'How, leave it up to her?'

Oliver was aware he was growling, but now a new gigantic worry had loomed up in his mind.

What if she wasn't excited about having a father?

What if she didn't want to meet him?

Keeping a scrapbook was one thing, but *meeting* her father...

CHAPTER SEVEN

EMILY's meeting with her father so far exceeded any expectations Clare might have had, that by the end of the weekend she was beginning to feel she was being excluded from a secret society.

Surely she couldn't be jealous of Em's delight in finding a father, nor feel put out that Oliver had slotted into the role with so much ease it seemed impossible the pair hadn't known each other forever.

Having delivered the news in the taxi ride home—incredible coincidence, maybe meant to be, et cetera—Clare shouldn't have been surprised to find that Em's first thought on arriving at the flat was to meet her dad.

'Can I call him Dad?' she'd asked, doubt in her eyes for the first time.

'You sort it out with him,' Clare had replied

as she'd knocked on the door, behind which, she guessed, stood a very anxious and uptight Oliver.

By the time the three of them had finished dinner—Em's favourite lasagne always cooked by Clare on Friday nights—together in Clare's flat, Emily and Oliver were chatting away like old friends, and the name *Dad* was falling easily off Emily's lips, and was seemingly as easily being accepted by Oliver.

Saturday they'd gone to the beach, then Saturday night to a movie Em just *had* to see. 'Does it worry you she seems to take such weird stuff as vampires and werewolves for granted?' Oliver had asked. So it wasn't until Sunday afternoon, not long before Em was due back at school, that the scrapbook came out.

'My gran did scrapbooking so she helped me put it all together,' Emily said shyly as she handed the carefully decorated book to Oliver. 'Gran says it will tell you the story of my life in pictures mostly, although there are words as well.'

Oliver was sitting on the couch in Clare's flat.

He seemed to have been there all weekend and his presence had been even more unsettling than the instant rapport the pair had achieved.

Now he patted the couch for Em to sit beside him, and with her by his side, pressed against him, he opened the book.

And frowned.

'That's when I was born,' Emily said, pointing to the first photo. It was a newborn-baby photo like a hundred others Oliver had seen, but it was the set of pictures on the other side of the page that had him frowning. These were pictures he'd seen before as well—a baby in a special-unit crib, tubes and monitor leads attached.

'Those are when I had my operation. I had a PDA. Mum said I needn't put those pictures in, but I think that's because looking at them makes her sad. But I don't remember and it was part of me, so me and Gran decided they should be there for you.'

'You had a PDA—you know what the words mean?'

'I used to know them,' his daughter answered cheerfully, 'but I forget. A little something went wrong with my heart and I had to have an operation—that's when Mum stopped being an actor and started being a perfusionist, because of my operation and learning all about babies with bad hearts.'

Oliver heard the words but his eyes were now on Clare. How could she have kept this from him?

How could she have not contacted him when *this* happened?

She must have read the anger and accusation in his eyes for she shook her head, just slightly, warning him to let it go for now, nodding to the new page open in the book which Emily was keen to show him.

He turned back to his daughter, banking down his anger, but determined to have this out with Clare later. She *could* have found him. He'd written enough papers that simply searching his name on the internet would have produced some hits.

'Are you looking?'

Emily's voice brought his attention back to the book, and looking at the pages, photos of his daughter as she grew older, the surrounds of each one decorated with small bears or balloons or pretty flowers, he felt such a surge of love for this child who'd done this for a father she didn't know that he forgot his anger and simply enjoyed the gift, not only of the scrapbook, but of a daughter.

The explosion came as they drove away from the school, leaving behind a little girl so full of excitement and delight Clare was worrying more about whether Emily would get sick with it, than any repercussions from the photos.

'She had a patent ductus arteriosus and you didn't think to tell me that before I met her?'

The accusation reverberated through the car, bouncing off the closed windows, unmuffled by the leather upholstery.

'We haven't had that much time to talk, and why tell you anyway? She had the op, video-assisted thoracoscopic surgery to tie it off. She's fine—I never think about it.'

Clare hoped she sounded calmer than she felt. Yes, she'd always discussed Emily's health with her mother, but she'd never had to answer to anyone for the decisions she'd made on Emily's behalf. Now, here was Oliver—who hadn't wanted a child in the first place—demanding full disclosure of his daughter's life.

'*Never?* She doesn't have ongoing specialist appointments? You didn't have her heart checked out before this riding business started? Are you sure she should be riding? Is it safe?'

Clare felt her own explosion building, and the tension of the past few days uncoiled in a flaming rush of words.

'Do you seriously think I'd put her life at risk allowing her to do something she's not fit to do? Where do you get off, walking into her life and criticising me, second-guessing my decisions? Of course she has regular check-ups, though only once a year now she's older. She's seeing Alex here, and yes, he did agree there was no problem with her riding. I'm not entirely stupid, you know!'

She paused for breath but her fury wasn't spent.

'Nor did I keep a daily health diary just in

case you might one day turn up in her life. She had whooping cough when she was two in spite of having had the immunisations. Do you want to know that as well? A greenstick fracture of her wrist at four, caused by falling off her bike when she persuaded Mum to take the training wheels off? What else?'

'You're being ridiculous now,' he growled, but Clare didn't care. The togetherness of the weekend had been bad enough, but now to have Oliver carrying on as if all that had happened in the past was somehow her fault was just too much. On top of that, she hated thinking back, especially to that period of time after Emily's birth, which was jammed tight with so many bad memories she tried never to think about it.

'*You* brought it up!' she snapped, the tension between them as palpable as the electricity in the air before a storm.

Oliver didn't reply, his silence intensifying the pressure in the atmosphere as they finished the short journey home.

He dropped her off in front of the flats and

drove off, Clare so relieved to be out of the car, she didn't care where he went. But just in case he was simply putting the car away, she fled up the path, unlocked the door and bolted up the stairs to the refuge of her flat.

Refuge? When she was listening all the time for the sound of a vehicle in the back lane, or the growl of the garage doors opening?

She had a shower, hoping hot water might ease the aching tightness their conversation had caused in her muscles. It was okay they'd parted as they had. Seeing how good he was with Emily had intensified the love Clare felt for him—but only by about a thousandfold. And after a weekend of such togetherness some traitorous part of her brain had been thinking maybe marriage wasn't such a bad idea.

A platonic marriage, of course.

Which would go down *really* well with Oliver!

But now she was sure he was sufficiently annoyed with her to have forgotten he'd ever suggested it, which should make her feel relieved, not uptight and disappointed.

And angry.

She turned off the water, wrapped a towel around her body, found a copy of Emily's health file and left it on Oliver's doormat, then made herself toast and jam for supper, and went to bed. She might not sleep, but at least with all the lights out Oliver might think she slept.

Or had gone out.

That thought made her think some more, her mind tracking along a completely new path.

His assumption that they should marry indicated he was assuming she had no social life at all.

Which she didn't, but that didn't mean he should assume it.

Could she conjure one up?

Pretend?

He had a daughter!

Oliver stood on the top of the cliff above Coogee Beach and looked out to sea, trying to assimilate the information, the reality of it.

Emily had been real enough when she was there—chatting so unselfconsciously, showing so little reserve to a virtual stranger, so childishly confident in the love of the adults she knew that she hadn't seemed to doubt for a moment he would love her.

He had doubted—oh, how he had doubted. Yet when he'd looked into those green eyes, familiar from the face he saw in the mirror every morning, something had swelled inside his chest, filling it to capacity, making him feel light-headed and woozy.

Stress, that's what he tried to put it down to, but her lack of awkwardness should have dispelled stress within seconds and that strange wooziness had remained with him all weekend, less all-encompassing but still there, swelling to maximum power again when she'd given him the scrapbook.

Was it love?

Could you feel love so instantaneously?

So intensely?

How could he know so little about love that he had to ask himself these questions?

Not wanting to think about the answer to that conundrum, he turned his attention to the future, except that thinking about the future meant thinking about Clare and, right now, thinking about Clare fanned the doused embers of his anger.

Logically he could accept that she had done her best to contact him when she discovered she was pregnant. Intellectually he could accept that not hearing from him, she would assume he didn't want to know his child, especially after the way they'd parted.

But the newly discovered emotional person inside him still blamed her and, blaming her, felt she was the one with the responsibility of sorting out where they went from here.

Because they *were* going somewhere.

All three of them.

The idea of being a part-time father was totally unacceptable. Emily deserved better than that. She deserved a family.

Oliver spun around and retraced his steps to the car. He needed to talk to Clare and he needed to talk to her now.

Clare was lying in bed, not even pretending to

sleep because her mind refused to settle, when she heard footsteps on the stairs.

Oliver was returning.

The footsteps hesitated on the landing and she knew he'd have found the file—the photocopy she always kept as they moved the original file from one specialist to another.

She hadn't left a note, just the file, but surely it was self-explanatory. Yet she didn't hear a key turning in his lock, instead there was a tap at her own door, then a louder knock.

Depleted of all energy from the emotionally fraught weekend, she didn't answer the summons. Let him assume she was asleep.

Or out?

She wasn't sure where the idea had come from, but suddenly the idea of avoiding Oliver for the next few days was intensely appealing. If she could just have a few days to herself—to go to work, come home and pretend life was normal—then by next weekend she might be able to think clearly enough to work out where they went from here in Em's relationship with her father.

It wasn't hard. Monday's operation was a complicated one that Alex and Angus were doing so she wouldn't have to see Oliver, and she knew Oliver was working Tuesday and Wednesday evenings, having swapped his weekend duty with Angus so he, Oliver, could spend time with Emily. Clare could go to the pantomime meeting without fear of seeing him there.

Thursday—well, she wouldn't get too far ahead of herself just yet, but if Monday's op was a long one, and there was no surgery scheduled for Thursday, she could probably take the day off and start on her Christmas shopping. She'd like to get something special for those nieces and nephews up in Queensland, and something extra special for her mother, who'd been such a rock in her life since Em was born.

Plans are one thing but, in reality, avoiding Oliver was difficult when he catapulted down the stairs behind her as she was leaving for work the next morning.

'Wait up. I want to talk to you.'

'And asking so politely too!'

Okay, so snapping at him was petty, but after

a week of unadulterated tension, she was desperate for a little Oliver-free time.

'It's about *our* daughter,' he growled, his voice telling her he probably wanted to see as little of her as she wanted to see of him.

She shrugged off the sniping comment.

'Was any explanation given for the PDA? According to the file she was slightly premature but four weeks is nothing these days. Did the paediatrician who saw her think it might have been genetic?'

Clare sighed.

'I really, really don't want to think about that time,' she muttered. 'You might not believe it, but it wasn't exactly a high point in my life. I've given you the file, what more do you want?'

She was striding up the road, trying not to get ahead of him but to escape the relentless awareness that stirred her senses whenever he was close.

'I want to know the nitty-gritty stuff. If we have another child, should we be prepared that this could happen again.'

'If we have another child?'

The words came out so loudly three pigeons nodding to one another on the roof of a nearby house took flight, the whirring flutter of their wings echoing in Clare's head.

Along with a lot of other confusion.

'Why on earth would you suppose we'd have another child? How's that likely to happen? Immaculate conception?'

He didn't touch her, but he was walking far too close to her, invading her space in a way she did and didn't like, her body and mind set on different paths.

'I told you I thought we should get married, and having met Emily I'm more convinced than ever that it would be the right thing for her.'

'For *her*?'

Forget pigeons, now she was causing the heads of the pedestrians waiting at the lights to swivel towards Oliver and herself.

'And what about me? Where do I come into it?'

Fortunately the lights changed so the pedestrians moved off the kerb while she and Oliver were still approaching, but she did mute her voice as there were people everywhere.

'We'd be doing it for Emily,' Oliver muttered at her, but it was too late—she'd taken off across the road, although the signal was already flashing. And with those words following her like a trailing streamer, she fled into the hospital.

She *had* to keep out of his way!

Oliver checked the patients in the cardiac PICU, then collected his outpatient list from Becky.

'I've got four more staff members from our unit willing to be in the pantomime,' she told him.

Pantomime? That's where his tumultuous week had really taken off.

'I'm only telling you because I know you're on duty Wednesday night and won't be able to make the meeting, but I'm sure someone will tell you all about it. And Friday night, there's a staff welcome party. I've put a notice on the board in the staff lounge. Alex likes everyone to be there because it's a chance to meet staff from other departments.'

'If I can't make it I'll explain to Alex,' Oliver told her, thinking that on Friday afternoon he'd be going with Clare to collect their daughter from school. Or was this Friday the party Emily had been chattering on about?

He'd have to ask Clare.

Given the rage she'd been in when they parted, this wasn't an appealing idea, but surely, eventually, she'd see the sense of his suggestion.

But asking Clare anything proved difficult when he couldn't track her down. From time to time, he did see her at the hospital, but never in a situation where he could discuss the very personal matter of their daughter.

'It will have to come out sometime,' he said when he did meet her in an elevator one day.

'What does that mean?' she demanded.

'Exactly what I said. Everyone will eventually know we have a daughter, so now she knows about me, would it be so bad if people overheard us discussing her here at the hospital?'

She threw him a glance that would have melted rock and exited the elevator, although he was sure she'd have no patients on the orthopaedic floor.

And catching her at home was impossible. He'd been on duty himself for two nights, and when he knocked on her door on Thursday evening there was no response. Unless she was living in the dark like a mole, she wasn't at home.

'Not that it's any of your business,' she told him coolly when he caught up with her on Friday and, rudely he supposed, asked her where she'd been. 'But there *are* on-duty rooms at the hospital, and there's been a very fragile baby on ECMO. Where else would I have been last night?'

Embarrassed, but still unreasonably angry, he was searching for a reply when her pager buzzed and she was whisked away. No doubt to the fragile baby on ECMO.

He could follow. He knew the baby in question and there was no reason why he shouldn't go into the cardiac PICU, but he also knew he'd be better off stepping back a bit, working out what was really upsetting Clare—apart from marrying him—before he blundered in again.

He all but growled. *He* didn't blunder. His relationships with women usually ran smoothly. They were well-planned campaigns, mutually satisfying, and ending in if not friendship, then definitely with accord.

Except, of course, his relationship with Clare.

Clare woke on Friday morning, aware her days of avoidance were over. This afternoon she would have to go home to the flat, to make sure things were ready for Emily for the weekend.

Thank heavens she'd had the forethought to ask Angus if he'd mind accompanying her to the staff party that evening, using the excuse that she hated walking into functions on her own. She'd sweetened the request by offering to buy him dinner at Scoozi first, and she hoped that Oliver might take the innocent outing as a date and so let go of the ridiculous idea that they should marry.

She shivered at the thought, aware after the

kiss they'd shared that while her body might ache for the satisfaction only Oliver could give it, the dark memories in her mind would always make her draw away from him.

Now she sighed.

Her heart had been telling her she loved Oliver—whether still or again—since shortly after he'd walked back into her life, but the reality of it was now gaining ground in her mind. And loving him, as she was reasonably certain she did, she couldn't possibly marry him. She refuted the damaged-goods label her head kept throwing at her, but she *had* been damaged, physically and emotionally, in the past, which meant she definitely wasn't good marriage material.

Oliver was contemplating knocking on Clare's door to ask her if she'd like to have dinner with him before the staff get-together when voices from the footpath made him glance out the window.

Clare and Angus?

Had they met by accident? Oliver was vaguely

aware that Angus also lived somewhere on this street, although closer to the hospital, he thought.

So why was he down here? Crossing the road with Clare? Walking into the park?

Oliver spun away from the window. What was *he* doing, spying on his neighbour like this?

The knot in his gut told him the answer. He was jealous. Jealous that Clare was walking and talking with another man.

And why?

He couldn't answer that one, but he knew it was unreasonable to be feeling like this. For all that he still thought they should marry for Emily's sake, Clare had walked out of his life a long time ago and was under no obligation to be faithful to him.

Not that he could assume she was being unfaithful with Angus—a man she barely knew!

And if that wasn't the epitome of confused thinking, he didn't know what was. He took himself off to the kitchen, fixed a toasted sandwich, ate it in front of the television news and told himself he wouldn't go to the party.

After which he told himself to grow up!

Poor Angus. Had their dinner conversation been as boring to him as it had seemed to her? Clare wondered about this as they entered the hospital, relieved when Kate joined them in the foyer.

'Your hair looks great,' Clare said, admiring the gloss and gleam of Kate's carefully straightened hair.

'Thanks,' Kate replied. 'It takes such an age to straighten, I don't do it often.'

And although not one cell of Clare's body had responded to Angus, good-looking though he was, she was suddenly intensely aware of him—of *his* tension.

Was he interested in Kate?

Had she, Clare, unintentionally bumbled her way into something she hadn't understood?

Confused and a bit embarrassed, she continued to chat with Kate about hair as they entered the elevator together.

Angus didn't follow!

'Are you with us?' she asked, and he moved in to stand beside her, although she was sure most of his attention was on Kate.

At the door of the function room, Clare realised she'd once again lost Angus. Kate had plunged into the crowd, but what was the point, Clare thought, of coming with Angus if they didn't walk in together?

She slipped her hand into the crook of his arm as they moved towards a cluster of their colleagues, ducking to avoid Christmas decorations, Clare muttering to herself about the tinsel but smiling at the team members.

Then not smiling as she realised Oliver was part of the cluster. But at least she had Angus as backup, for all he seemed to be very distracted.

They stood and chatted for a while, Oliver disappearing as Becky told a doctor joke, then Angus, too, drifted off. Clare took a drink from a tray and looked around the room, hoping it appeared that her gaze was wandering casually over the throng, rather than looking intently to see where Oliver had gone. She was considering another circuit when her heart gave an excited little blip and she realised it was the back of his head she could see, over by the buffet laid out for their supper.

But in spite of the urge to talk to him—so much for keeping her distance—wouldn't it look too obvious if she just wandered over there?

Angus was not far away, so she'd grab him first.

'Let's go get something to eat,' she suggested, and although Angus looked slightly startled— he'd seen the dinner she'd eaten—he fell in with the plan.

So he could see Kate, who was also by the buffet?

Clare shook off the confusing thoughts and took Angus's hand, all but dragging him along.

'Well, hi, you two—fancy meeting you here.'

Was she making a point? Oliver wondered. Why else was she holding hands with Angus?

Or was she using him as a shield? Protection?

'I knocked on your door,' he said as she drew close.

'I left early,' Clare replied, their conversation so stilted it hurt her to think they'd come to this.

Kate was talking about taking their supper up onto the roof, suggesting all four of them went.

'Won't it be windy up there?' Clare protested. 'It'll blow your hair.'

Kate shrugged off the comment, but before Clare could speak again, Oliver had made the decision for her.

'Well, I'll keep an eye on Clare for you while you're gone,' he said, probably to Angus, although Clare was sure the words were also meant for her.

She shouldn't have avoided him all week. Avoidance didn't solve anything, especially when there were things of major importance to sort out.

They were adults. They could discuss things rationally.

Well, almost rationally—just standing near

him right now was sending all the wrong messages to her body.

'Can *we* go somewhere and talk?' he asked, speaking her thoughts and so confusing her a little more. Was he feeling what she was feeling? Would this talk be personal?

'About Emily?'

He shook his head, answering two of her questions, one asked and one unasked.

'About you,' he said, then he reached out and tucked a swatch of hair behind one ear. 'About you,' he repeated, but so softly it was little more than a breath of air puffing from his lips.

'We can't leave yet,' she managed, although now he'd asked she wanted nothing more than to talk to Oliver, to let out so much of the poison she had bottled up inside her. Once he knew about her past he'd stop pressing her about the marriage thing and they could have a good relationship with each other and their daughter.

'But soon,' he said, then he turned away as Alex tapped him on the shoulder, asking him to come and meet a surgeon from the general ward.

Clare watched him go. She was aware of feeling nervous yet relaxed—two diametrically opposite emotions existing side by side within her.

She chatted to various members of the team, met people from other wards and disciplines, but was aware all the time of Oliver's presence in the room, as if her sensory receptors were tracking every move he made.

'So, now can we leave politely?' He came up to stand behind her, and she turned towards him, smiling as she nodded her response.

Oliver doubted he'd ever been as aware of anyone in his life as he was of Clare through that seemingly endless evening. Was it her beauty that stirred him so deeply, the outward serenity of her even features, the tumbling mane of hair, swept up off her neck tonight, though tendrils had escaped to trail against the golden skin?

She slipped her hand inside his elbow, his arm crooking to tuck her fingers into place.

'Didn't you have a date?' he asked as they wove their way towards the door.

She raised dark eyebrows at him.

'Been spying on me?' Then she shrugged. 'I came with Angus. I asked him, not the other way around. It was stupid—infantile—thinking if I avoided you we wouldn't have to talk, but Em deserves we do the best we can for her, so maybe if we get all the talk out of the way we'll see a path ahead more clearly.'

'What kind of talk?' Oliver asked cautiously. They were alone in the foyer outside the reception room, most people still enjoying the hospitality provided.

She pulled a face, gave another little shrug.

'The other night—I can explain...'

But she was looking pale again so he put his arm around her and ushered her into the elevator, keeping his arm there so she was tight against his side.

'Let's wait until we get home,' he murmured, nodding to the people entering on the next floor down.

She didn't argue, but he could see the lines strain had drawn on her face, and feel the unhappiness tightening her body.

What could he do to ease her pain? At least alleviate it slightly so the walk down their road wouldn't be so agonising for her. They were back to ground level now, and the foyer was as busy as it always was.

But usually—

'Here,' he said, and drew her into one of the small rooms that were part non-denominational chapels and part simply quiet spaces where people could release emotions and regain their fortitude before facing again some of the horrors they had to deal with in a hospital situation.

And in that private space he kissed her, not passionately, but gently, carefully, trying to tell her without words that he was there for her. She nestled closer, not responding to the kiss intensely, but responding nonetheless.

Was it because this room had held such emotions that images of how Clare's life must have been seemed to flash across his mind? First discovering she was pregnant, not hearing from him, hurt beyond words that he should care so little for her news—alone with her misery at what should have been a time of excitement and delight. Then Emily's birth, alone again, and frightened, when she discovered her baby had a problem.

He folded his arms around her and held her close, not kissing now, but wanting to say so many things.

'You need never have to face things alone again,' he murmured against her hair which was tumbling down from its clasp and feathering against her shoulders.

She snuggled closer for a moment, then drew away, lifting her hand to touch his cheek.

'If only it was that easy,' she whispered, then she took his hand and led him out of the room. 'Let's go home. We'll talk there.'

CHAPTER EIGHT

FOR a flat that had much the same furnishing as his, Clare's place was so distinctly different. It had the feeling of a home, something he'd never achieved in any of the rented apartments he'd had over the years.

He didn't for a moment believe that only women could make a place homely, so…

'I guess I never really cared about where I lived, not in the sense of wanting it to offer anything more than shelter and a certain amount of comfort and security,' he said as Clare led him into the living room and continued on to throw open the bay windows.

She turned and looked at him, eyebrows raised in query.

'This place—I didn't take much notice at the weekend, with Emily here—but it looks homely,' he explained.

'You mean messy and untidy,' Clare said, coming forward and picking up a magazine from the arm of one chair and tossing it into a wicker basket on the floor by the couch. 'Call it rebellion, or perhaps it's just the natural outcome of having a child around the place. There is always stuff hanging around.'

Oliver nodded. He could see the evidence of Emily's existence, a handpainted card on a side table, a hair ribbon tied to the stem of the large-leafed plant in one corner of the room, a butterfly on a stick stuck into a smaller pot plant on the windowsill.

But though these snatches of his daughter's life caught his eye, his mind was back on the first thing Clare had said.

Rebellion.

'Rebellion?'

He repeated it out loud and saw her shoulders lift as she took in a deep breath.

'Do you want coffee or tea, a drink? I have some wine, but no spirits.'

He shook his head.

Another deep breath, then she gestured to the armchair.

'Then let's sit down. I have to tell it from the beginning or you won't understand.'

She threw him a half-smile before adding, 'Actually, you might not understand anyway. Most of the time I don't myself.'

Clare watched Oliver sink down into the comfortable armchair, then seated herself on the couch, drawing up her legs under her, almost unconsciously making herself as small as possible.

Less of her to hurt?

'When I left you, I went home to the farm. It was only a week before Christmas, you remember. Everything was fine. I mean, I was miserable, but the family were all kind and supportive and I pretended to be okay. Both my brothers were still living at home, and my sister, who'd shifted to Queensland, was down for the festive season, and life went on. Then one day Dad fell down.'

'Fell down?'

Clare paused, recalling so vividly that day in

the dairy when her father had seemed to trip and fall, but then had failed to get up.'

'Apparently he'd been feeling lousy for a while, but being Dad hadn't said anything. Mum had noticed he was dragging one foot but when she asked him about it he brushed her off. It was Christmas—everyone was busy, but cows still had to be milked. With Dad only half there we all dug in and got through, then in the New Year, Mum insisted he see the doctor.'

This was where the telling became difficult, Oliver realised, and knowing how much Clare had loved her father, he got out of the chair and came to sit beside her, not touching, just being there.

'Eventually,' she said, nodding as if accepting his move, 'he was diagnosed with motor neurone disease—right about the time I diagnosed myself as being pregnant.'

Clare had told him this bit looking down at her lap, toying with a button on her skirt. Now she looked directly at him.

'You'd know about MND. In most cases it progresses very rapidly. We all wanted Dad at home because we knew he'd be happiest there, so although Liz went back to Queensland, I stayed on at the farm to help out. Steve's mate Barry used to come three or four days a week to give a hand with the milking. He'd changed to beef cattle so was free. I contacted you and didn't hear, but there was so much emotion flowing around the place, Oliver, that not hearing from you was just one more thing to set at the door of unkind Fates.'

She offered him a smile, but he could hear the pain of those days in the huskiness of her voice and see it in her tortured dark eyes. He ached to touch her, to hold her, but something in her stillness warned him off. The glass wall was there, and though he suspected it was fragile, he didn't want to shatter it right now.

'We moved Dad into a hospice the week before I gave birth to Emily. Mum was staying there with him, and while by then I wasn't much use to the boys around the farm, I could still help out by shopping and cooking. When my waters broke, four weeks early, Barry was there, having called at the house to drop off a couple of casseroles his mother had made for us. He took me to the hospital and he stayed there with me. Mum couldn't leave Dad, and my brothers were busy at the farm, so Barry stuck around. He was wonderful. Just having someone there when I was told about Em's PDA, just having someone to lean on—I was so grateful to him.'

Oliver stood and strode across to the window, aware *he* should have been the one supporting Clare, so aware of it the awareness hurt.

Yet how could he have been there? How could he have known?

He stopped himself grinding his teeth just before he did damage to his tooth enamel, but the anger and frustration inside him was almost too much to bear—especially as Saint Barry was now front and centre in Clare's thoughts.

'So you married him?' Oliver found himself growling. Better that he ground his teeth but he couldn't stop the words from bursting forth.

Huge dark eyes studied him—unreadable in their intensity.

'Not then,' she finally whispered. 'First I

tried to find you, then Dad died. Mum was devastated—lost. Em had her op, and the boys sold the farm. I had to stay in Victoria as Em was still seeing specialists and *then* I married Barry.'

Oliver assimilated the words. Really assimilated, for they seemed more to seep through his skin and into his blood than enter through his ears. And with them came the pain Clare must have suffered, the gut-wrenching loss of a beloved father, the fearful news that her newborn daughter had a heart problem, the isolation when her family moved away.

Damn the wall! He reached for her and drew her close, holding her as he would hold a hurt child, offering comfort, nothing more.

Clare melted against him, the tension of the telling of the story draining out, the warmth of Oliver's body so seductive that for a few seconds she imagined maybe everything would be all right.

Could she pretend that was the end of things?

Would Oliver accept that one failed marriage

was enough to put her off the institution for life?

Probably not, but she was all talked out for one evening, and sitting like this, with Oliver's arms around her, was so close to heaven she didn't want to move, or think, or do anything much at all.

Just sit and let the bliss of it wash over her.

Just sit and not think at all.

But life didn't allow time for such luxuries. Oliver was turning her in his arms, slipping his fingers beneath her chin, turning her head, so she had to look at him.

Or so he could kiss her?

A deep shudder ran through her body, quickly relieved when his lips moved to speak, not to kiss.

'The marriage didn't work?'

She considered shaking her head, then knew she needed to say the words.

'The marriage didn't work,' she repeated, and this time knew he must have felt the shudder for his arms tightened around her and his head lowered so he could drop soft kisses on her hair.

So comforting. So very, very comforting.

But unacceptable! She was probably giving Oliver false hope about the marriage idea.

She eased herself away from him, pushed her hair back off her face, pulling it into a bundle and knotting it out of the way.

'I'm sorry, but getting rid of all that pent-up emotion has exhausted me,' she said, and watched his face, wanting to see some reaction, but reading nothing in it, or in his green eyes.

All he did was nod, then he stood up off the couch and walked towards the door, pausing there to ask, 'I take it we can go together to collect Emily in the morning. We can go in my car? What time?'

Clare frowned at him, unable to believe she'd been towed so far back into the past that the present—including her daughter—had gone completely from her mind.

'We can collect her at nine, which means leaving here about a quarter to.'

She knew she was still frowning, but that was

because she realised she needed some time away from Oliver, the intimacy of telling him about the past now weighing heavily on her.

But she'd tried avoiding him last week and avoidance hadn't achieved a thing. They had to forge a way forward together, to find a life that would be stable and enriching for their daughter.

'Are you okay?' he asked, still hesitating in the doorway. 'Do you want me to stay?'

He smiled at her.

'Even to stay as a friend, not a lover?'

'I'm fine,' she lied as love for this man she was turning away swept through her, shaking her so badly she needed him to leave so she could sit down alone and put herself together again.

Emily was tired and cranky. A rainy afternoon during the week had meant she'd missed her riding lesson; the party had been gross.

'That's terrible,' Clare translated for Oliver's benefit.

'The music was really lame,' Emily's plaint continued. 'Dad, can I have a guitar?'

As Em was sitting in the front seat next to Oliver, Clare had no chance to send a silent signal to him that guitar ownership had already been discussed and knocked back.

'I'll have to talk to your mother about it,' Oliver replied, and Clare gave him a tick of approval.

Emily produced a theatrical groan.

'Mum'll say no, I know she will. She'll say I'm already having riding lessons and I'm playing soccer and when would I have time to practise and what's the point of having one if I don't practise?'

She mimicked Clare's voice so well Clare had to hide a smile. They were driving down the back lane, the garage door sliding up in response to the remote, so Oliver had an excuse not to reply, though he did say, 'Ah!' in a thoughtful voice.

'I've got an old guitar back home in Melbourne, hardly used,' he said to Clare while Emily had found Rod sitting in the garden and was telling him about her week—sounding far more excited about it than she had when telling her parents.

'Should I get it sent up for her?' Oliver finished.

Clare shook her head.

'Let's wait and see,' she suggested. 'She might want a flute next week.'

Then she smiled at him.

'Got a flute tucked away at home?'

Oliver looked at this woman who had been through so much, yet could still smile and joke and carry on as if life was the great adventure she'd always thought it. Something quivered inside his chest—not attraction for sure—something far more subtle than that.

Something he didn't want to think about.

Emily had joined them, bouncing up and down with excitement.

'I asked Rod if he'd come and talk to my class at school about being a writer and he said yes,' she announced.

Oliver looked across at Rod, who nodded and smiled.

'I love talking to kids about writing,' he

admitted. 'They're so full of enthusiasm. Clare, can you organise a time with the school, perhaps check they really want an old man like me coming to visit?'

Clare moved towards their landlord and bent to kiss his cheek.

'Of course I will and thank you,' she said, then she straightened and looked at her daughter. 'Em, you've got your key? How about you take your things upstairs, then get a cup of tea going for Oliver. I'll be up shortly and we'll sit down and plan our weekend.'

Emily stood her ground.

'Are you going to tell Rod about Dad?' she asked, and Oliver wondered by what intuition a nine-year-old could fathom such a thing. He'd guessed that's why Clare was lingering in the garden, believing it was only right that Rod should know what was going on with his tenants.

'Come on,' he said to his daughter. 'What your mother wants to talk to Rod about is none of our business.'

The green eyes flashed towards him, rolling

in a manner that said, Not you too, without the words, but Emily led the way around the side of the house, dug her key out of her overnight bag and opened the doors.

'The girls at school thought it was weird that I suddenly had a father,' she told him as she stomped up the stairs. 'They wondered if I'd change my name.'

She reached the landing and turned towards him, face-to-face as he was still a few steps behind her.

'Will you and Mum get married?' she added, the simple innocence of the question stealing Oliver's breath.

'Let's get that cup of tea going,' he told her eventually, 'and work out what we want to do over the weekend. Have you ever seen horse races? I thought we might go this afternoon, not so much to see who wins the races but so you can check out the thoroughbreds as they parade around the ring. Would you like that?'

'Could I have a bet?'

It was the last question Oliver had expected

and he frowned at this apparently knowledge-able small person who'd come into his life.

'What do you know about betting?' he de-manded, and was rewarded with a cheeky grin.

'Melbourne Cup of course. *Everyone* knows about the Melbourne Cup! The teachers even let us watch it on the television because they say it's part of the Australian culture.'

Put firmly in his place, Oliver repeated the question. Would going to the races interest her?

'I'd like to see the horses,' she told him, head-ing for the kitchen and lifting the electric kettle to fill it with water. 'Because they brush them somehow so they have patterns on their rumps and I'd like to learn to do that for when I have my own horse.'

Oliver rather doubted she could get horse-grooming lessons at the races, but he liked the idea that he'd thought of something that might interest her—that he, not Clare, had come up with the outing.

Clare.

He took the kettle from his daughter and filled it for her, although she assured him she could manage.

Was he fiddling around in the kitchen so he didn't have to think about the trauma of Clare's life in that year after they'd parted, so that he didn't have to feel, well, guilt that he hadn't been there for her?

The story had spun around in his head as he tried to sleep the previous night, and snippets of it—things he wanted to ask about—kept coming back to him.

'I'm going to change. Mum has her tea black,' Emily announced, apparently happy to leave him in charge in the kitchen, though she'd no sooner left the room than she reappeared. 'Do I wear going-out clothes to the races?'

'Perhaps we'd better consult your mother before we decide definitely that's what we'll do,' he told her, and she frowned ferociously at him.

'I thought a man could decide things like that on his own,' she said. 'Anyway, Mum won't mind. She likes horses too. She used to live on a farm, you know.'

Before Oliver could work out a reply to this conversation, Clare appeared.

'I explained to Rod,' she said briefly, then she turned to Emily. 'You're not changed yet?'

Emily heaved a theatrical sigh.

'Dad says we can go to the races, but we have to ask you first, so I don't know if I should put on going-out clothes, or beach clothes or what.'

'Go to the races?'' Clare echoed faintly. Bad enough that she had to give their landlord a brief explanation of their convoluted relationship, but now, apparently, she had to make a decision about going to the races.

'It'll be fun,' Oliver said. 'Here, I've made the tea, and I've told Emily we won't be betting, just going to look at the horses and we needn't stay long.'

Unable to think of a valid reason for *not* going to the races when it was put like that, Clare nodded at her daughter.

'Going-out clothes, something cool, and the hat Gran gave you for your birthday.'

Emily skipped off into her bedroom and Clare sank down onto the stool in front of the kitchen bench.

'The races?' she said, looking at Oliver across the tea things.

'She likes horses,' he said, though he looked so embarrassed Clare had to smile.

'Have you been thinking all week of outings you could offer her?' she asked. 'We don't have to go out, you know. She can just as easily spend the weekend at home, with a high treat being a walk across the park for a pizza at Scoozi for dinner.'

Oliver nodded, but still looked put out.

'I suppose it's because I've missed so much of her,' he said, 'that I feel I should be making up to her all the time.'

He paused, then he reached across the bench and touched Clare lightly on the cheek.

'Making up to you as well,' he added softly.

Clare felt the touch. It felt like love, although she knew it was sympathy and understanding.

She wanted to grasp his fingers and hold them to her cheek, but his hand had moved away already, and besides, it would have been unwise.

'I'll go and put on some going-out clothes,' he said. 'I imagine we can get lunch out there. Shall we say leaving here at eleven-thirty?'

Clare nodded, her mind already scooting off touches and love and delving feverishly into her wardrobe.

Going-out clothes?

She didn't go out.

She had one kind of all-purpose black dress she'd worn the previous evening, suitable for everything from dinner parties, to hospital functions, to funerals. But going-to-the-races clothes?

She dashed across the landing, banging on Oliver's door.

'I haven't got any going-out clothes.' She all but wailed the words, catching herself in time and trying to sound like a reasonable adult. 'I don't want to disappoint Emily, so how about you take her?'

Oliver looked at Clare for a moment, then

shook his head. He left her on his doorstep while he walked across into her flat, knocking on Emily's door.

'You decent?' he asked, and the door opened to reveal Emily already dressed in a pretty but simple sun frock that had been part of her birthday present from Gran.

'Your mother hasn't anything to wear,' Oliver told the child. 'Where's the nearest place we can buy going-out clothes for her?'

'Ooh, can I come too? Can I help you choose? The shopping centre just up the road has a boutique with some super grown-up women's clothes. I've been telling Mum for ages she needs to buy some decent gear. She came to the school my first week in jeans and a jacket she bought in Chicago—can you imagine?'

Clare slumped against the doorjamb and shook her head in bemusement. Between them, her daughter and her daughter's father were disrupting her life so much she wondered if she'd ever get it back on track.

But within minutes she'd been swept off between the two of them, and hustled into a boutique, where Emily darted around pointing to clothes she thought her mother should buy, while Oliver sat down in an armchair obviously provided for male companions, and gave every indication that he was ready for a show of some kind.

Not that Clare intended parading in front of him, although once she had a pretty patterned skirt and top on, she was so unsure of how she looked—so unused to seeing herself in going-out clothes—she did actually go out of the changing room to ask him what he thought.

She looked so nervous and uncertain Oliver's first instinct was to take her in his arms, but knowing that would be disastrous in a shop, *and* in front of Emily, he studied the outfit.

'You look fantastic in anything,' he told her, 'and those colours look great on you. Are you happy with the two pieces or would a dress be easier?'

By now Clare was looking distinctly embarrassed, and when she muttered something about a skirt and top being more practical because she could get more wear out of them, it made him wonder if maybe she had no going-out clothes because of financial restraints. He had no idea how much she earned, certainly less than him, and with school fees and uniforms and riding lessons and rent…

'Try on the other things and show me, then we'll decide.'

'Try on the brown spotty dress first,' Emily put in, then she came and sat beside Oliver on the arm of the chair. 'She never buys anything for herself,' she confided to him. 'She says it's because she doesn't need to, that she has enough clothes for work and weekends and that's all she needs. Mum's idea of dressing up is putting a jacket over her jeans and polo shirts.'

It was an artless conversation but Oliver was struck by the enormity of what had happened because his mother, out of pure spite, didn't forward on a letter. For ten years Clare had struggled on her own, or with whatever help her mother could give her, while he'd never hesitated to buy the latest laptop, or a new Italian suit, or take a skiing trip in the Alps.

He wanted to buy her everything in the shop,

to fill her life with the things she'd been deny-ing herself. He wanted to marry her and take care of her for ever so she never had to scrimp and save again.

She came out in the brown dress with the white spots, and he stopped thinking altogether, his mind numbed by the vision in front of him. The dress was probably fairly ordinary as dresses went. It was made of some silkily soft material so the skirt swirled softly around her long legs, while the V-neck of the top showed the shadow of her breasts, the whole effect breathtaking.

'Told you it would be super,' Emily said, leaping up from the arm of the chair to dance around her mother. 'It *is* super, isn't it, Dad?'

Oliver found it hard to respond. It was indeed super, but the beauty of this woman had taken his breath away and his mouth was too dry for words.

'Well, that's okay, but I can't buy it anyway. I can't wear black sandals with it and that's all I have, so I'll get the skirt and top which are more sensible anyway. I can wear the two pieces separately, mix and match.'

'With your jeans!' Emily groaned in a long-suffering voice, rolling her eyes in mock disgust at the same time.

'Well, the top would look good with jeans,' Clare said crossly, and she disappeared back into the changing room.

There she sat down on the little stool and tried hard not to cry. The brown dress was so classically cut and elegant, she'd felt a million dollars in it, but it was the look in Oliver's eyes when he'd seen her in it that had really struck deep into her heart. He had looked at her as if she was beautiful and for a moment she had felt beautiful—something she hadn't felt for a long time.

And wanting that feeling to last, she really wanted the dress, wanted to walk beside him in it.…

Being maudlin will get you nowhere, she told herself sharply, standing and carefully removing the dress, returning it reluctantly to its hanger. She put on her own clothes, then carried the skirt and top out of the changing room to find her daughter and Oliver had disappeared.

'They said to wait,' the store attendant said. 'I'll just get the dress from the changing room.'

'I'm not taking it—just these two things,' Clare told her, but the woman bustled away, returning with the dress and putting it down on the counter.

Emily's excited voice told Clare the others were returning, her daughter bursting through the door with three pairs of sandals in her hands.

'Try these on, Mum,' she insisted. 'Dad said the least he can do is buy you a pair of sandals when he hasn't been con—'

She stumbled on the word and Oliver put in 'contributing' for her, so Emily could finish her explanation.

'—contributing to my clothes or school or anything. If you get a pair of sandals you can buy the brown dress which looked super on you.'

Emily hustled her to the chair Oliver had used earlier and knelt to slip off her mother's sneakers, replacing them with delicate, strappy sandals.

'Perfect,' she said, and Clare had to laugh—her daughter a saleswoman at nine.

'Try on the others as well,' Oliver advised. 'You might like one of the other pairs better, or you could have all three.'

'No-one needs three pairs of white sandals,' Clare objected, and now the saleswoman got involved.

'Hush your mouth!' she said sternly. 'You'll be struck out of the fraternity of women if someone heard you say that.'

Clare smiled as a happiness she couldn't remember feeling for a very long time welled up inside her, bubbling like a spring freed from some obstruction.

'I'll take this pair,' she said, choosing the sandals she'd first tried on, then she looked up at Oliver. 'You don't have to do this, you know,' she told him, but all she got in reply was a short shake of his head before his attention turned to Emily.

'Come on, kid,' he said. 'We'd better get these

back to the shoe shop and pay for the ones we're taking.'

He turned aside to speak to the saleswoman, while Emily gathered up the shoes, keeping the discards in one hand and the pair they were to buy in the other.

'Back soon, Mum,' she said, then she dropped a kiss on her mother's cheek. 'Isn't it fun having Dad around?' she whispered, and suddenly the spring of happiness wasn't bubbling quite as high.

Clare knew Oliver's reasoning behind the gift of the sandals and—it appeared when she went to pay—of the clothes, and though she felt awkward about accepting such things, she would do it graciously. But Emily's whispered comment had hurt her in a way she didn't fully understand.

She knew it wasn't jealousy she was feeling, but disappointment of some kind—disappointment that the life she'd been providing for her daughter hadn't measured up....

'Hey!'

Oliver had returned and was standing beside

her, and his hand rested lightly on her waist as he murmured the word.

'We're going forward, remember. Just enjoy Emily's delight.'

Clare nodded, wanting so much to be a full participant in this new family of three, but knowing it could never be, not the way Oliver wanted it.

They returned to the flats where Clare changed into her new finery, eliciting cries of delight from her daughter.

'You need my pearls, the ones Gran gave me,' Emily declared as she inspected her mother for the last time. 'Wait here.'

She ran off to her bedroom and returned with the pearls that had been her great-grandmother's, making her mother sit on the bed so she, Emily, could fasten them.

'There,' she said, 'you're beautiful. Dad will surely want to marry you now.'

Clare knew the words were nothing more than childish enthusiasm, but once again the joy of the morning dimmed, and despair wormed its way into her heart.

How could she resist if it became a matter of two against one?

How could she deny her daughter life in a family situation—two parents living together, not in separate flats?

She shook her head, knowing she couldn't resist or deny, yet knowing she couldn't marry Oliver either.

CHAPTER NINE

THE afternoon at the races was an unqualified success. Emily was fascinated by the patterns on the horses' rumps and totally infatuated by the beautiful thoroughbreds.

Clare felt like Cinderella, decked out in fancy clothes, knowing all the time the ball would end and she'd be going back to the reality of her life with only minor changes.

'I don't intend to talk to you about things tonight, with Emily around,' Oliver said to her when they returned home after eating dinner at a Chinese restaurant near the racecourse. 'But tomorrow night—we'll sort it all out then.'

He paused, possibly listening for sounds from Em's bedroom, for the little girl had been tired enough to head straight to bed.

Then he continued, 'She asked me if we'd get married, did you know that?'

Clare stared at him, unable to believe Em had spoken that way to a man who, for all he was her father, was still virtually a stranger to her.

'She's only nine. It probably seems to her the kind of thing adults do. She's no idea what marriage really means, or what being married might entail for the two people involved. All she wants is a mum and dad at home like other girls at school, although statistically speaking there are probably as many different home situations as there are girls in her class.'

Oliver studied the woman he'd decided he would marry, the woman he'd been so proud to have by his side this afternoon, the woman who appeared, on short acquaintance, to have done an excellent job of bringing up his daughter.

'We'll see you in the morning,' she said, telling him the conversation was over for this evening, but his thoughts stayed with him as he made his way into his own flat.

He knew Clare still had feelings for him. He'd seen it in her eyes from time to time, when she thought he wasn't watching her, yet she held to this stubborn resistance against their marriage.

It wasn't lack of attraction—that still ran strong between them, so strong that even standing close to her he could feel it thrumming in both their bodies.

So why?

Because she felt the failure of her first marriage was her fault?

Because she was afraid she'd fail again?

The Clare he'd known had been afraid of nothing. Well, maybe snakes, but a lot of people had an atavistic fear of snakes. But she'd had no emotional fear, throwing herself into love as wholeheartedly as she'd plunge into the ocean on a hot day.

Ah! Was it *his* fault? Had their split made her cautious about loving again? Had he hurt her so badly she feared to love again?

Useless speculation! They'd talk tomorrow evening, after they'd dropped Emily back at school, and in the meantime he'd read about a great restaurant on the rocks beside the beach at Bondi, not far from where they lived. They could all three go for breakfast there, then wander through the Sunday markets, have a swim and be home in time to do whatever Clare had to do to get Emily ready for her return to school.

He pulled out his mobile and dialled Clare's number, telling himself he was phoning her to make these suggestions to her, not because he wanted to hear her voice just one more time before he went to bed....

Togetherness crept up on you, Clare decided when once again they were in Oliver's car, heading for Emily's school. Em was chatting on to Oliver about all the things she'd have to tell her friends when she arrived, turning to ask Clare if she could invite one of the country girls home next weekend and to remind her to phone the school about Rod coming to talk.

The wonderful breakfast at the beach, the walk, the swim, had all left Clare so pleasantly tired she agreed with everything, although she knew when she got back to the flat she'd have to write herself a note about phoning the school—about Rod and about the boarder coming to visit.

When she got back to the flat.

Would they *have* to talk?

Could she plead exhaustion?

She thought not, although it would be real enough. She was usually tired after a weekend with Em because they always tried to pack as much as possible into it, but tonight it was emotional exhaustion.

It weighed her down and dogged her footsteps as she walked from the car to the front door of the house, then up the stairs, making every step an effort.

'Too tired to talk?' Oliver said when they were both on the landing.

She nodded, then shook her head.

'No, let's not put it off any longer,' she mumbled, tension twining through her body as she said the words, tightening as she led him into the flat where she dropped onto the couch, but in the middle so he couldn't sit beside her.

Not that it stopped him. He sat and edged her along, then put his arm around her.

'Of course we can put it off,' he said, so gently she felt like weeping. 'There are better things for lips to do than talking anyway.'

And with that he kissed her, so softly at first it was barely the brush of skin on skin, the touch of a rose petal.

But it was never going to be enough, his mouth moving against hers, testing and tasting her lips, his tongue exploring, not delving yet, but teasing her so she responded with her own tests and tastes, melting against Oliver's body, revelling in the feeling of being held not tightly but securely in his arms.

The heat she'd been trying to hold at bay crept through her body once again, and desire so strong she wondered if it would overcome all else sang in her blood. His lips devoured hers now, hungrily seeking deeper and deeper responses, responses she was happy to give.

Mindlessly she floated on a sea of sensation— being in Oliver's arms, kissing Oliver and being kissed by him—time and troubles fading into oblivion while remembered bliss tweaked her nerves and coursed through her body.

Oliver had gripped her hair, tugging gently so her head fell back and his lips could find her neck.

Did every woman have erogenous zones along the line of the blood vessels in the neck, or was it only she who shivered with delight when his lips pressed against her skin, and his tongue delved into the hollows where neck and torso joined?

His mouth was moving lower, buttons sliding open on her shirt, her hand against the back of his head, feeling the roughness of his hair.

Oliver!

She was twenty-five again—no, twenty, when all of this was new and exciting, when kissing Oliver was an exploration of a whole new world of sensation. His tongue slid into the deep cleavage between her breasts, increasing the longing in her body, so she pressed against him, nibbling at his ear, sucking on the lobe, sliding her tongue into the hidden whorls, feeling his reaction in his hardening erection.

It would be all right, she told herself. This

was Oliver. She was safe. It would be fine. She needed love; she wanted it, wanted him.

Wanted him?

The words began to echo in her head and were blotting out the wonderment kissing Oliver had provided.

'Oliver!'

She breathed his name, and although she knew it must have taken a superhuman effort, he pulled away from her, still holding her, but not tightly, to him—not kissing her.

'I can't do it,' she whispered, her voice hoarse and her body shaking. 'I'm not teasing you—I thought I could, but I can't.'

He sat there, looking at her, no expression at all on his face.

So many explanations, none good, were racing through Oliver's mind he couldn't speak. He couldn't react at all. Something was very badly wrong here and until he knew what it was he couldn't begin to think about it, let alone do anything to make it right.

His immediate reaction to this second rejection had been anger, but that had been his libido talking. One look at Clare's face told him every word she said was true. She *couldn't* do it!

And there was no need to be coy about it and pretend he didn't know what 'it' was. They'd both been so worked up sex had been all but inevitable.

All but.

He took her hand in both of his and looked into her beautiful and unutterably sad and weary face.

'Can you talk about it?'

She shook her head, then bent it so her hair hid any expression from him.

'I thought I could do that as well, but now…'

So what to do?

She needed him—or someone. He knew that as surely as he knew he loved her, though why that revelation struck him right now he didn't know. He could hardly say it at the moment; she'd think he was using it as a weapon—something to force the issue of whatever it was she was hiding.

So he sat and held her hand in his, waiting,

barely thinking, but willing to sit there all night if that's what was required.

So her movement startled him. She snatched her hand away, straightened up and looked directly at him. Then, holding his eyes, she ripped open her shirt and wrenched her bra aside, revealing her full and beautiful breasts, as proud and upright as they'd been when she was ten years younger, but—

Scarred?

He stared, unable not to, at small white lines like snail tracks, and bruised knotted tissue.

'Oh, my darling,' he whispered and took her in his arms again, holding her, not knowing what to say or do, except to hold her, murmuring now of love, telling her— talking, talking, talking, while her silent tears soaked his shirt.

Had she really stripped off her shirt and bra? Shown Oliver her scars? How *could* she have done that? How utterly embarrassing? How on earth was she going to face him in the morning?

Worse, how had she ended up in bed? Her last

memory was of sitting on the couch, saturating Oliver's shirt with stupid, senseless tears, while the poor man talked of love, no doubt to try to stop her crying.

Clare clambered out of bed, pleased to see she was wearing her knickers, though nothing else, and headed for the shower, hoping to wash away the disjointed memories and get her mind into work mode once again.

But as she stared at the toast she'd made, and tipped her coffee, untasted, down the sink, her stomach squirmed at the thought of seeing Oliver again, working with Oliver today, pretending that nothing untoward at all had happened between them.

She left the flat, escaping. As far as she remembered Oliver was doing a PDA today, the same operation Emily had had, tying off the little duct that before birth carried blood between the arteries but after birth was supposed to close. No heart-lung machine required, but she wouldn't be at Jimmie's anyway; she'd been asked to assist at a hospital across town where a complicated adult operation was taking place.

Following the instructions the perfusionist at the other hospital had given her, she caught a train to town, changed there to another line, then felt a surge of delight as the second train took her on the famous bridge across Sydney Harbour, the wondrous sight of the Opera House down below. She'd been promising Emily a trip to the centre of the city to take in these sights, but they'd finally decided to leave it until Em had Christmas holidays so they could possibly stay a night in town.

'He's been on a ventricular assist device,' the perfusionist explained when Clare had been shown to the theatre and introduced to the man she'd only known as a voice on the phone. 'But as no heart has become available—rare blood group so it's going to be hard to find one—we're going to take out the old device and put in a more modern version of it, one we think will make him more comfortable.'

Having worked with teams putting these devices that helped the heart beat into adult patients in Chicago, Clare was only too happy to assist, but things went horribly wrong when the old pump was disconnected and it was discovered that the man's blood vessels were so damaged attaching a new device would be difficult.

'Heart surgeons can do anything!' the lead surgeon announced with more bravado in his voice than he must have been feeling.

Clare watched the monitors on the heart-lung machine, in sole charge now as the other perfusionist worked with the surgeons to find viable blood vessels in the man's chest.

'Maybe an external pump,' one of the surgeons suggested, but the lead man shook his head.

'The whole idea of doing the op was to give the man better quality of life. Is tying him to a hospital bed for however long it takes to find a heart a better quality of life? No, we'll do this. We might have to put in stents from good tissue in the blood vessels, and connect the stents to the LVAD.'

Clare checked the clotting factor of the man's blood, and the oxygenation, checked all the pumps were working, worrying about air bubbles now the man's chest had been open for so long. Then, eight hours after they'd begun, the job was done. She'd been spelled from time to time, forcing herself to eat and drinking coffee by the gallon, but now that the man was in the hands of the regular perfusionist and the anaesthetist, the weariness of the long hours in Theatre all but overwhelmed her.

'We've plenty of duty rooms you can crash in,' one of the nurses, perhaps sensing her exhaustion, offered.

'I think I might do that,' Clare told her. 'I don't think I could face the trains at this time of night.'

The nurse summoned an aide who led Clare along strange corridors, eventually opening the door of a typical on-duty room.

'There are toiletries in a sealed package in the cupboard—not much choice, male or female—and some theatre pyjamas if you want something to sleep in. Help yourself to tea or coffee or anything you might find in the refrigerator, but check the use-by date on any sandwiches. Who knows when the fridge was last stocked up.'

Food was the last thing on Clare's mind. She collapsed into bed, only to be called at four. They were taking the patient back to Theatre and, as the first perfusionist had been with him all night, could Clare assist?

'I've let Jimmie's know you're still here,' the head theatre sister told her when she joined the team in the theatre once again. 'Thank heavens you opted to stay the night.'

The team worked swiftly, knowing the man's life was already at risk. This second operation in twenty-four hours put strain on his entire body, not just his failing heart.

The surgeons spoke quietly, suggesting options, discussing and dismissing them while they removed the device they'd inserted the previous day.

'Maybe an external pump is the only answer,' one said.

'We still have to connect it to his heart, and to do that we have to connect it to blood vessels, and that's our problem—finding a couple that can take the pressure.'

But eventually they did it, although Clare stayed around until midafternoon, afraid if a blood vessel began to leak they'd have to open the man's chest again.

'All good!' the lead surgeon finally declared. He turned to Clare. 'You can go back to your babies now,' he said, 'but thanks for the hand and thank Alex for lending you to us. I know how tight your team is, so lending someone out is a strain on everyone.'

Clare was feeling too weary to do more than nod acceptance of the man's kind words. She changed into her civvies, pleased she'd washed out her undies and they'd dried while she slept, and caught the train back to the city, dozing as they crossed the bridge, changing trains, then finally arriving at the station just across the road from the rear of Jimmie's grounds.

It was only as she stared at the place that was fast becoming so familiar to her that she re-membered it was Tuesday—rehearsal day for the pantomime.

Feeling certain that Oliver intended dropping out and not sure if anyone else from the cardiac team would turn up, she muttered the age-old words—*the show must go on*—and made her way to the canteen in the second tower.

Fate was apparently still in its capricious mood for the first person she saw was Oliver. In fact, she probably saw a lot of people before him but he was certainly the first to stand out in the crowd.

Tables had been pushed back and an area representing a stage marked out on the floor. Dr Droopy was clutching a bundle of paper, and Clare realised with some surprise that they had moved as far as scripts.

Oliver had seen her come in and now he made his way, unobtrusively he hoped, towards her. He didn't know why, given how angry he'd been to find she'd disappeared on him again. Not having seen her all day at the hospital, he'd knocked on her door last evening. No reply.

His immediate reaction had been fury. Damn the woman! He understood why she'd avoided him the previous week, but once she'd decided to tell him things, surely she shouldn't have been hiding herself away again? His anger had burned through the night, so he'd felt foolish—even ashamed of himself—when Alex had explained Clare was on loan to another hospital.

He didn't doubt that the tension he'd been feeling since he'd seen her scarred breasts had fired the anger, which, in retrospect, was more against whoever had hurt Clare than against Clare herself.

So with all this turmoil messing his head, he finally came to stand beside her in the small throng of people Dr Droopy was already calling to order.

'I've decided against the separate performances but still want people from all of the wards to do guest appearances therc. Even if it's just a wander through the wards in costume a couple of times, it will make all the children feel included. The main performance now will be much bigger and grander and I've some preliminary scripts here for you to take.'

There was general muttering among the cast,

but Oliver's attention was on Clare, who looked pale and tired.

'Rough op?' he asked, resolutely refraining from putting his arm around her and giving her a hug.

She offered him a weak smile.

'Two of them, both rough, and there's no telling if the poor patient is out of the woods yet.'

'We can only do so much,' Oliver was telling her when Dr Droopy stopped in front of them.

'You're the cardiac lot, aren't you?' he said.

'That's us,' Oliver responded, wondering what had happened to the other four Becky had mentioned.

'Good,' Dr Droopy told them, then he consulted his list. 'Clare Jackson, right?' he said to Clare, who nodded.

'I want you for Snow White.'

'Snow White isn't in *Cinderella*,' Clare objected.

'It's panto,' Dr Droopy reminded her. 'I thought as we were only doing the one performance—though probably two or three times—I'd put a lot of other nursery characters into it. With the ball scene we can have whoever we want there.'

'Makes sense,' Clare told him. 'The little kids these days seem to know the name of every princess ever written. My daughter certainly did.'

'How old is she?' Dr Droopy demanded.

'Snow White?' Clare was frowning at him now.

'No, your daughter! I'm after mice. Could she be a mouse?'

Clare hesitated but Oliver stepped in.

'I'm sure she'd love it,' he said, then he turned to Clare. 'She'll be on holidays soon, so will be able to come to rehearsals.'

Clare gave him a look that suggested there'd be further discussion on the subject later, but she didn't object. In fact, she offered Emily's name to the pantomime director.

'And you,' Dr Droopy continued, turning to Oliver, 'will be the fairy godmother. I thought

I might get someone really ugly to begin with but we can do wonders with make-up.'

Oliver began to protest but as Clare was laughing and it seemed so long since he'd heard that delightful sound, he shut up.

The other clowns passed scripts around, and a rough read-through began, but Oliver's attention was more on Clare than the familiar words being read out in different voices—on Clare and the hurt she had suffered, presumably at the hands of her ex-husband.

He knew enough to understand the physical scars were probably the least of her worries, that the emotional scars would be the ones that took longer to heal—might never, in some cases, heal.

But what could he do?

How far into her space would she let him intrude?

'You look exhausted. I'll get a cab to take us home?' he said as the rehearsal broke up.

'A cab home? It's just down the road, Oliver. I'm not made of glass!'

True enough but Clare *did* feel fragile. That

was the natural outcome of a combination of little sleep and the emotional outpourings of Sunday evening. But the feelings of acute embarrassment she was now conscious of in Oliver's company were worse than any tiredness.

Shouldn't she have simply told him she'd never marry again? Couldn't she at least have kept him at arms length? But to show him the scars, to reveal herself that way, not so much physically—although, oh, boy, did she ever do that—but emotionally as well? Had she been crazy?

They left the building together, Clare careful to walk far enough away from him they didn't accidentally brush against each other.

'Come and eat with me,' Oliver suggested as they went up the stairs to their flats. 'I'd actually intended asking you yesterday and bought some chicken pieces. I do a mean Moroccan chicken.'

Clare tried to smile. The idea of Oliver cooking—not just a grilled steak and chips but from a recipe—was enough to make anyone who'd known him smile. But she'd lost her smiles somewhere and the best she could manage was a shake of her head.

'You *will* come,' he told her. 'You will sit down, have a glass of wine, leaf through a newspaper or watch something mindless on the television while I cook, then eat and go home. No talk, no pressure, Clare—I promise you.'

She heard the sincerity in his voice and, when she looked up, saw it mirrored in his eyes.

'I don't deserve you should even speak to me,' she whispered, and the softness in his eyes vanished as anger blazed in its place.

'You will never say that again!' he said, icy words slicing through the sultry summer air. 'You are deserving of so much more than me, deserving of the best of everything. You are beautiful and kind and good. You're an excellent technician with a top-class reputation. You are a woman our daughter will always be proud to call her mother, and one she can aspire to be like.'

Clare stared at him, then felt her throat thicken, but she refused to cry again. Swallowing the lump that threatened to choke her, she said a simple, 'Thank you,' then sank down into Oliver's armchair and stared into space.

Oliver's words replayed themselves in her head and she knew they were a gift she could never repay. Knew also that they might spell the beginning of an ending for the past. Oh, she'd got beyond her marriage break-up, forged a career and made a life for herself and her daughter, but deep inside she knew she'd never grown emotionally, never healed the scars that weren't visible.

Could she heal with Oliver's help?

Not when he'd promised not to pressure her.

When he'd promised not to touch her...

Tired as she was, she stood and walked towards where he was chopping things in the kitchen.

'Can you put it all away and order pizza later?' she asked him.

He looked up, so obviously puzzled that now she had to smile.

'Why?'

She came around the bench to stand beside him, and reached up to kiss him on the lips.

'I want you to take me to bed.'

He put down the knife but otherwise didn't react, silence stretching tautly between them.

'You're exhausted. You haven't thought this through,' he told her, brushing his fingers against her cheek. 'Sex is the last thing you need.'

'Yes to the first, but no to the second and third. I've done nothing but think about it ever since we met again. I've thought about whether I could go through with it, whether I'd let you down, whether you'd be so repulsed you wouldn't want me.' She hesitated, then continued, 'Please, Oliver, I really want to do this, but if you find my...my scars...off-putting, then just say no and I'll never pester you again.'

Oliver couldn't speak, so he wrapped his arms around her and held her close, smelling hair shampoo and garlic from the recipe, his mind churning at a million miles an hour.

What was she really asking?

Why now?

She was tired and vulnerable; could she handle it?

His body thought it was a great idea, but then his body was so obsessed with her it had thought cooking dinner for her was a reason to tighten.

His brain was still throwing up questions when she pushed away from him, far enough to look into his eyes.

'I'm not asking you to do this as a kind of medicine—you know, a cure of some kind. I'm asking because if we're to even contemplate a future together we have to know if I can do it. Do you understand that?'

That's when he saw the fear and knew the effort it was costing her to make this suggestion, to give herself to him.

'I understand you are offering me a gift beyond price,' he said, his voice rasping out of a thickened throat. 'You are offering me total trust, my darling woman, and that is so special I feel unworthy.'

He lifted her into his arms as easily as he might lift Emily, the gift she'd given him instilling power as well. In his bedroom he set her down gently on the bed, then knelt beside her, leaning down to kiss her lips, her eyelids, her brow and temples, then her lips again. His hand moved to her shirt, unbuttoning it, his fingers running across her chest, her belly—gently, softly, barely brushing her skin.

Still kissing her, he undid the snap on her jeans and slid the zip down, his hand delving further now, fingers tangling in the curls, seeking the moist lips beneath them.

They moved on the bed, adjusting to each other, he shedding his trousers and shirt, while Clare tugged off her jeans and top. He didn't touch her breasts, although later he would—later he would have to, to show her without words how beautiful she still was.

For now it was enough to feed their arousal with lips and fingers, exploring and remembering, Clare's hips lifting in encouragement as his fingers slid inside her. She stilled, and held him tightly, and he felt her muscles spasm once, again, and then relax. A sound that was little more than a whimper whispered from her lips, then she guided him into the slick depths and they moved together, remembered rhythms raising the excitement until Oliver could bear no more and spent himself inside her, her sigh of quiet delight suggesting she'd also enjoyed release.

They broke apart and she curled into him, but he knew they weren't finished. Holding her against his body, he undid the clasp on her bra. At first she stiffened, then, although he could feel reluctance in her muscles, she allowed him to remove it.

Now he knelt above her again, straddling her but keeping his weight off her body. He turned on the bedside light and dimmed it to its lowest setting. With his eyes on hers, he bent his head, and kissed first one breast, then the other.

She lay motionless beneath him but he could feel her...if not fear, then trepidation. With infinite tenderness he let his lips follow the lines of the scars; he kissed the tiny puckers, and lapped around her peaking nipples, forcing himself to relax, reminding himself that this was now and this was for Clare and she didn't need more anger in her life.

'Beautiful,' he murmured, taking one nipple

gently into his mouth, teasing at it with his tongue.

She stiffened, then relaxed, beginning to move, to use her hands against his skin, exciting him again, as if to tell him she was now enjoying his attentions.

'Are you sure?' he asked as her fingers coaxed excitement from his body.

'Oh, yes,' she murmured, and this time as he plunged inside her the cry of release was loud and heartfelt, her muscles clasping and releasing, draining him completely.

CHAPTER TEN

THEY lay together, still joined, and haltingly the words came out.

'He was so good, so supportive, the whole time Em was in hospital, then he told me he'd bought a farm of his own. We'd have our own place—Em could grow up in the country as I had.'

She paused and Oliver rubbed his hands across her back, massaging the muscles he could feel tensing beneath her skin.

'I don't need to know,' he said.

'I need to tell,' she whispered.

'He said, let's sell your car and buy a newer dual-cab ute, safer for the baby than my old ute or your old car. Mum had bought a baby capsule and we used it in my car to take her home. It was close to Christmas and he'd decorated the house with tinsel. I cried to think he'd done that just for me. Later—maybe just a day or two, I can't remember now—he took my car to town to buy the new ute. Ordered it, he said, but coming up to Christmas it might take a while.'

She paused and snuggled closer, and Oliver found his arms tightening around her.

'The house on the farm was old, but I didn't care. I planned to do it up, bit by bit. He liked it tidy, liked things neat, so I was happy to have things to do. It was isolated, you see, but with Em to care for and the house, it didn't seem to matter.'

Her voice was growing quieter, as if whispering the memories might somehow make them less horrifying.

'Sometimes, when Em had been fretful and things around the house hadn't got done, he'd look around the messy room and sigh. Not saying anything but I'd feel that I'd disappointed him. Then one day, we were about to go to bed, and Em woke for a feed. It must have stirred his jealousy, and it triggered something in him I'd never have guessed was there.'

Anger so deep and hot he wondered he could

keep it capped seemed to boil within Oliver, but he realised that, now she'd started, Clare needed to go on. He could only hold her, aching for her, fearing what he was about to hear, wondering if he could maintain his control.

'The new ute never came. I couldn't leave the house because we couldn't put the capsule in his old vehicle. He picked up groceries when he went to town. Sometimes he'd have a drink while he was there and after that would be rough with me—squeeze my breasts too hard. Mum had sent a box of Christmas decorations, some old ones I'd loved as a child and new ones, too, for Em's first Christmas, although we knew she was too small to know. I cut a little tree in the bush not far from the house and decorated it. It was Christmas—everything would be all right.'

She was shivering now, remembering, and Oliver could do nothing but hold her close and listen as the poison of that time was lanced from her soul.

'But Christmas meant parties, not that I'd go. I wouldn't enjoy them, he'd say, and besides, how could we take the baby? He'd meet some mates and have a drink and that was when he hurt me. He was always sorry afterwards, always promising it would never happen again, but one night, sometime in January, he grabbed my breasts and scratched them with his fingernails, scoring them and pinching me so hard I had to muffle my cries in the pillow in case I woke Em and he hurt her.'

Oliver felt her face pressed hard into the curve of his neck and knew his skin was wet with tears.

Was there more?

Could he listen to more?

Control his urge to find this man and murder him?

Then Clare's whispered words began again and he had to strain to listen.

'I realised just how jealous he was of my baby, of my feeding her, of my giving her any attention at all, and that's when I knew I had to leave. I waited until he slept, and knowing he'd been drunk so he'd sleep deeply, I took the capsule and Emily and left, walking not along the road but across the fields. The neighbours all around knew us both—knew Barry better and liked and respected him—so I had to get as far away as I could, carrying Em in the capsule because I knew I'd need it if I found someone to give us a lift.'

Oliver heard the words, so flat and emotionless, but in his mind he saw the woman he loved, trudging across the fields on the peninsula southwest of Melbourne, and he felt the fear she must have felt, the agony of desperation.

And understood her courage.

'I had a school friend in a small town near Apollo Bay. It was morning by the time I got there, so I went to her place. She didn't ask a single question, just put me and Emily in her car and drove us to the airport, paid for my ticket to Queensland on her credit card, bought some food and coffee for me, and once I was safely on the plane she phoned Mum to meet me at the other end.'

'Did he look for you?'

Oliver was surprised his voice had worked, so choked up did he feel.

Clare nodded against his chest.

'But not for long,' she whispered. 'Both my brothers flew south to see him. I don't know what happened but they came back and told me he wouldn't bother me again. Later Steve apologised, saying he had no idea Barry could behave that way. Apparently when they'd arrived, Barry had shown them the pile he'd made of my and Emily's clothes and all the gifts she'd been given. He'd put the Christmas tree and decorations on the top. He'd soaked them in petrol and had apparently been waiting for an audience for he set fire to it in front of them.'

'He was mad,' Oliver muttered. 'He must have been.'

Clare kissed his cheek.

'I thought so for a long time,' she said softly, 'but in the end I think perhaps he was just obsessed. For some reason I'd become the object of that obsession.'

She shivered and Oliver held her close again, murmuring not sweet nothings now, but talking of her courage and his love.

Thinking a pizza delivery after midnight

might disturb Rod downstairs, Oliver made scrambled eggs and toast, coaxing Clare to eat until her body realised it needed fuel and she ate the lot.

Once she was fed, he took her into the shower, where he soaped her body, washed off the soap, dried her down and tucked her back into bed, his bed—Clare as docile as a child, allowing him to take care of her, although maybe she was so emotionally spent she could do nothing else.

He lay in bed beside her, knowing he should sleep, but wondering about how she might wake up in the morning, not wanting her to feel uneasy or embarrassed that she'd bared her soul to him.

'It was a gift without price,' he whispered to her when she did awake, sitting up uncertainly on the side of the bed.

'Making love?' she queried, a little frown puckering her forehead.

He shook his head and smiled at her.

'Telling me,' he said. He sat up, kissed her lips, then patted her lightly on the back. 'Now we've got to get to work. Tonight we'll need to catch up on our sleep, but by Thursday we should be rational enough to talk about where we go from here, okay?'

She was still frowning, so he kissed her again.

'No more today,' he told her. 'Don't think about the past or the future. Let's get to work— there are babies to be helped.'

Now she smiled, and Oliver's heart scrunched as if a giant fist had gripped it hard.

Was it love?

It had to be.

Clare wrapped his robe around her and dashed across to her flat to prepare for work, while Oliver moved into the bathroom, realising as he showered just how vulnerable love made a person.

It held you hostage, trapped you—yet the face in the mirror was smiling at him, so could it be all bad?

Obedience seemed the safest course. Clare kept her mind on the day ahead as she dressed for work. One of the things she loved about her work was the uncertainty of it, not knowing what case they might have to deal with next.

Oliver tapped on her door as she finished dressing. She called to him to come in, still feeling slightly anxious about the welter of emotion she'd dumped on him during the night. But when he kissed her, not with heat but with what felt like love, she put the past behind her, and delighted in his company even if all they were doing was walking to work together.

They went first to the PICU, where Oliver introduced her to the baby whose PDA he'd fixed on Monday. The baby's mother was in a chair beside his crib, dozing while her infant slept.

'You might have missed Em growing up but don't regret missing all the worry that went on when I discovered she had a problem,' Clare told him as they left the unit, knowing there was a team meeting in ten minutes. 'You feel so helpless, so useless, and although you know your child's in expert hands, not being able to do anything yourself is incredibly frustrating.'

Oliver squeezed her shoulder, just as Becky

emerged from her office, heading for the meeting room.

'Aha,' she said. 'Cupid strikes again!'

'We're old friends,' Oliver told her, surprising Clare as they hadn't at any stage discussed how they'd handle their relationship at work.

'Oh, yes?' Becky said, eyebrows rising and a teasing smile lighting up her face. 'And don't think you're the only ones. Have you seen how Angus looks at Kate?'

Clare shook her head. She wasn't into hospital gossip, but usually if there was something going on within a team as small as theirs, there'd be some kind of buzz.

'Too absorbed in our own reunion,' Oliver whispered to her as Becky dashed away, 'but now Becky knows, the whole world will. Does it worry you?'

He turned to look at her, his green eyes showing his concern.

Clare pondered it for a moment, then shook her head.

'Not that we're going to stand in a team meeting and make an announcement,' she said, 'but no, if people begin to realise we're together, then that's okay.'

She stopped and studied him again, aware she must be frowning.

'Oh, dear, that's assumption on my part. Just because you were kind to me last night—it needn't mean more than that, Oliver, truly it needn't.'

She was looking so harried Oliver had to re-assure her, dropping a light kiss on her lips in spite of their location in a hospital corridor.

'Except it does,' he told her firmly. 'I love you, Clare, and probably always have. I've wasted ten years of both our lives, and in doing that I put you into a position where you were alone and then abused. I can never make that up to you, but from this day forward I will do everything in my power to help you forget that time. I just hope my love for you will be strong enough to do that.'

'Am I interrupting something important?' Alex asked, edging past them in the corridor.

'Yes,' Oliver told him, putting his arm around

Clare's shoulders to steer her up against the wall. 'We'll be with you in a minute.'

He'd intended kissing her, right there and then, but Kate was coming, and Angus, and the junior surgeon, so he made do with a brush of his fingers across her cheek, then led her into the meeting room where the entire team was awaiting their arrival, a smile on every face, and speculation in their colleagues' eyes.

Circumspection meant they kept to their own beds on the weekends when Emily was home, but every other night they spent together and, safe in the cocoon of bed and darkness and Oliver's love, Clare let out the pain and anguish of her brief marriage, then told of how she'd remade herself, determined for Emily's sake not to be a victim, and not to let the past drag her down.

Oliver would hold her and marvel at her strength and courage, unable to believe his love for her could still increase every day. With Emily, they shopped for Christmas decorations, Emily insisting they wait and buy a real tree,

Oliver insisting they do without tinsel in their plans—so tacky, he said to his daughter, winning a warm smile from the woman he hoped to soon make his wife.

Two days before Christmas, the three of them turned up for the final performance of the pantomime. Oliver had only done one stint as the fairy godmother, having to do an emergency operation on the afternoon of the first one. But tonight he was back; in fact, both the fairy godmothers were there, and their jealous behaviour towards each other had the audience laughing with delight.

Emily had made friends with the other mice and had spent the previous night with one of them, Mia, the daughter of a nurse in the orthopaedic ward. With the performance over, the small Emily mouse bounced up to Clare and Oliver, who were still in costume as they planned to do a visit to the wards.

'Mia and I decided we'd be bridesmaids when you two get married,' she announced. 'And Mia said the right way to propose, Dad, is to get down on your knees—or maybe one knee, I don't remember now—but if you're going to do that, can I watch?'

'Can we all watch?' a deep voice said, and Clare turned to see Dr Droopy standing right behind them, and behind him most of the cast.

And now she looked around it seemed the audience had stayed on as well, surely not expecting more of a performance. But before she could speculate further, the fairy godmother— grotesque make-up, wig, huge fairy wings and all—was down on one knee, reaching for her hand, asking her to marry him.

The cast and audience applauded and the mouse jumped up and down, then Oliver was on his feet, taking her in his arms, enfolding her and Emily, encompassing them both in his love.

'Did Snow White really marry the fairy god-mother?' Clare heard a child's voice ask.

'In fairy stories anything can happen,' some-one responded, but Clare was beyond caring what other people thought. She had her own happy ending right there.

MILLS & BOON PUBLISH EIGHT LARGE PRINT TITLES A MONTH. THESE ARE THE TITLES FOR APRIL 2011.

❧

NAIVE BRIDE, DEFIANT WIFE
Lynne Graham

NICOLO: THE POWERFUL SICILIAN
Sandra Marton

STRANDED, SEDUCED...PREGNANT
Kim Lawrence

SHOCK: ONE-NIGHT HEIR
Melanie Milburne

MISTLETOE AND THE LOST STILETTO
Liz Fielding

ANGEL OF SMOKY HOLLOW
Barbara McMahon

CHRISTMAS AT CANDLEBARK FARM
Michelle Douglas

RESCUED BY HIS CHRISTMAS ANGEL
Cara Colter

0411 Rom LP

MILLS & BOON PUBLISH EIGHT LARGE PRINT TITLES A MONTH. THESE ARE THE TITLES FOR MAY 2011.

HIDDEN MISTRESS, PUBLIC WIFE
Emma Darcy

JORDAN ST CLAIRE: DARK AND DANGEROUS
Carole Mortimer

THE FORBIDDEN INNOCENT
Sharon Kendrick

BOUND TO THE GREEK
Kate Hewitt

WEALTHY AUSTRALIAN, SECRET SON
Margaret Way

A WINTER PROPOSAL
Lucy Gordon

HIS DIAMOND BRIDE
Lucy Gordon

JUGGLING BRIEFCASE & BABY
Jessica Hart

Discover Pure Reading Pleasure with

Visit the Mills & Boon website for all the latest in romance

Buy all the latest releases, backlist and eBooks

Find out more about our authors and their books

Join our community and chat to authors and other readers

Free online reads from your favourite authors

Win with our fantastic online competitions

Sign up for our free monthly eNewsletter

Tell us what you think by signing up to our reader panel

Rate and review books with our star system

www.millsandboon.co.uk

 Follow us at twitter.com/millsandboonuk

 Become a fan at facebook.com/romancehq